I0822701

ALICIA NICOLE NORMAN

Where Do Black Girls Go To Cry?

IhG

INTERNATIONAL HOMEGIRLS.COM

First published by International Homegirls 2019

First edition

ISBN: 978-0-692-19770-7

Editing by Julie Doar-Sinkfield
Editing by Nadia Casseus-Torney
Editing by Santina Brown

This book was professionally typeset on Reedsy.
Find out more at reedsy.com

To Black Girls.

Mom, I did it.

To Patrick

To King Aidan

To my Homegirls...

Permission To Cry

Allowing this single tear to run down the side of my oiled face is somehow, therapeutic.
Powerful even.
This single tear is a child of war by its origin.
Heavy with the weight of Mother Earth, this tear is only beginning its descent upon the fires of hell.
Descending to extinguish its wrath.
its true purpose not revealed, crashes with Earth.
Blinks of reality initiate its intent. Sometimes you must stop trying to convince yourself that you are alright.

- Alicia Nicole

Contents

Foreword

I wrote each letter as each tear fell. Unsure of each word I penned, I wiped my eyes for clarity. I lifted my head from the pen and paper sitting, disheveled on my lap. I was uncomfortable in the driver's seat of my little car. Maybe my seat was up too close to the steering wheel because I began to feel claustrophobic. It's hot but my gas tank is almost empty, and I'm broke with no money, so I can't really afford to be running the car just for the air conditioner. Hell, I don't even have a place to lay my head tonight. I need to be worried about that instead of writing this letter.

If you'd experienced firsthand, my life, with all of its ups and downs, turnabouts, forks in the road, and bridges out due to icy roads ahead, you would have killed yourself too. I don't know how I let myself get this out of control. I thought I had a handle on this depression and anxiety thing. I don't and it is out of control now and I can't handle life anymore. I don't know which me to be. I doubt every move I make. My soul is ready to explode from the cages of my body, ready for freedom. Not just for me, but for us all.

Many years ago, I thought I knew who I was going to be. Funny, my answer, when anyone asked me what I'd be when I grew up, was never alone and never dead before 35. I never thought that I'd see the day when I gave up on myself. My grandmother told me once, "you not supposed to ever let yourself down." Today is that day that I disobey one of my ancestor mothers. I'm tired of fighting.

I'm sitting in a parking lot in my car with the radio on, writing you this letter. I'm writing you this letter, so you'll be able to tell my story. I won't be here when you get this but at least you'll know why I did it. I didn't have anyone I could call. No friends, no family. No one that would really understand. My depression has caused me to totally isolate myself from the world.

I've gone so long being on my own that it's become my normal. I turned my phone off so I wouldn't burden anyone with my personal problems. I'm aware, everyone has their personal battles in life and issues that could cause self-destruction at the drop of a penny. It would be selfish of me to make them carry my problems along with what they are already responsible for carrying.

I'm sitting in my turmoil, deciding how to end my life. I'm tired and I can't take living like this anymore. That's why I'm leaving you this letter. When I'm gone, tell them I tried, I just wasn't strong enough. How many times can you knock yourself down then stand up again? These are self-inflicted wounds, I know, but they still hurt. I'm wiping tears as I write this. This car is all I own. No big house. Nothing. I came to this place to escape my responsibilities. I came to this place to cry. I think I came to kill myself. If they ask, tell them, "She had to die so that she could live."

I didn't grow up thinking I was supposed to do anything special. I never thought I'd impact anyone's life. Never even desired to. I didn't think of myself as different from the pack or better than anyone. All I knew was that I was Rochelle. I cared not about how anyone else behaved unless it directly affected me. I could care less what people looked like or what they wore. I had no competition because I never considered myself to be in any type of sport or game. I was no competitor. This was never a race to me. I was so carefree, it's laughable to think about it now. Or Sad.

As I reflect on my life and everything I endured. I wish I could get that child back. The one with the ponytails, bangs, braids and beads. She was innocent. Naive. It was her innocence and naivety that was her strength. Fear was foreign to her, but it also became her downfall. Becoming someone who everyone else considered to be the Black Sheep, was inevitable. Not because I wanted anyone to see me that way but more so, because that's the category they put me in once I started reaching for my goals. I always stood out without trying. I've often wished I could follow my purpose, be me, while being invisible at the same time.

The dreams I had, how I behaved, my thought process, none of this seemed normal to anyone but me. I learned over time that I was different. I spoke my mind. I wasn't afraid to learn new information, to travel, to be genuine. Keep in mind, I never considered myself different. That's what they said about me. Said it so much that "different" became a negative term. Words have power but tone and intentions are the driving force. I've heard them say "She thinks she's better than everyone else. Why is she so Different?" I can't escape this. I've learned to dim my light a little now. I've learned to blend in and adapt. I know how to hide even if there are only three of us in the room and the room is as big as a kitchen pantry.

I can make you see exactly what I want you to see when you look at me. Makeup and hair weave help hide the real me. This way I only show you the parts of me you can handle. I don't want to call any unnecessary attention to myself. So, I have mastered the art of deception. Don't think for one minute that this means I become quiet or fade into the background. Quite the opposite. My loudest voice has become my camouflage. I can conceal my true self with the image of the outspoken, life of the party, that I give to people. No one gets the real me anymore.

Time teaches lessons. The lesson I learned the most? No one was ready for the real Rochelle. So, I kept her hidden, tucked away inside me. She lived there. Inside my head. I've lived inside my own head for as long as I can remember. I haven't had a very difficult life by most standards. It's been years of effortless progression until I gave up on myself recently.

See, I was the little black girl whose mother wanted her to succeed, whose father wanted her to be happy, who's siblings would at least pretend to like her in front of company. I was the little black girl who walked through life, lost, when everyone assumed I was found. I don't know if that makes sense. I don't know if any of this will make sense. I'm just talking to you. I'm trying to tell you how I ended up in this parking lot contemplating suicide. Planning for suicide. Preparing myself, for suicide.

There, I've said the word. I feel sick to my stomach. Everything I didn't eat today is coming back up like vomit but there is none. The thought of killing myself is a weak man's way out in my family. We just don't do shit like this. I never really ask myself how I ended up here. Why I hit this low. I know the answer. I wonder more why it took me so long to get here. I wonder why I've never snapped before; with all I've been through. I wonder how I've never snapped before today.

In 30 years, I have lived a plethora of lives. I've lived as many different versions of myself or of someone I thought I should be..., adapting to my environment. Assimilating. Camouflaging. Molding myself into the person I pretended to be, reacting to the road bumps of life. Always becoming. Never actually being.

Each year of my life, that I can recall, I was someone different. I had folded myself into so many pieces that the creases of me became the layers that defined me. I lost myself or I never really knew my real self. Always playing a role as if I was the starring character in a Broadway musical. In this musical, I play the girl with a perfect life, who knew all the answers, and who was good at everything she attempted to do. She is beautiful. She wears a long weave, likes yoga and practices meditation. She's confident. She is a friend to all. She doesn't get attached, knows what love is, and freely offers it up to anyone in need. She has all her shit together. She can run a successful business, is talented beyond measure, and she handles her financial responsibilities.

Nothing could have been further from the truth but just like a chameleon, I blend easily, and I played my role perfectly. Always remaining in character. I was so good at pretending to be someone I really wasn't that I fooled myself into thinking I was the woman I pretended to be. When reality set in, I was the starring character in something that seemed much more like a horror story. It was much worse than it sounds. I never even stopped to think about how wrong it was to live so many different lies and lives or how this type of thinking and behavior was not normal. Most people just lived as one person. I never considered the damage I was doing to myself. How adapting to situations verses creating my own situations and choosing my standards, and morals, beforehand, made me more of a victim of my circumstances.

I never had control of my own life, I only pretended to have control. I have the habit of blaming people, making them responsible for the choices I make. I conditioned myself to think and to be this way. I made a pact with myself that if I lived this way, I would be somehow, protecting my true self. Shielding myself from anyone looking to cause confusion, hurt or pain in my life. All of this sounds absurd considering I came from a very strong and loving family. My aunts and uncles seem so sure of themselves. I envy them. My mother and father, still married to this day, able to protect and provide for not only themselves but for their children who are now adults. They live, my parents, as if they've found the answers for questions, I haven't even learned to ask yet. I feel lost in this world of people where everyone else already knows exactly where it is that they belong.

I'm an ant in comparison to the women in my family who are elephants. They take care of themselves, their families, and they all work their asses off. My mind just doesn't allow me to live like that. I'm super emotional and I give up on everything when it gets difficult. My gene code requires me to be able to handle any and everything without completely falling apart and shame on me if I give up. This is my mind again fighting with my brain, revealing my insecurities, turning my dreams and desires into nightmares and new-found fears.

I should be stronger than this. I tell myself, yet, nothing changes. Deep down somewhere I've known for a while that I should seek professional help. I do not function as a normal adult should. The way that I think and prioritize life is awkward, but I'm a strong black woman and if things really get bad, I can always take my problems to the Lord in prayer. These were the words of every Black woman before me. This is the code they lived by.

Mostly unspoken, the Black girl code implies that each member of the black girl club be educated, loving, selfless, beautiful, remain presentable up until bedtime, allow all others to speak their minds as we quiet our own so to not seem angry, become leaders in every area humanly possible, have children, raise them alone, hold down your family, hold down a job, eat right, grow amazing hair, and overlook all of societies traps set in advance, specifically to ensure our failure.

I think that's exactly what landed me here. I'm still trying to make sense of it all. It's important to me that you understand why I decided to take this path. I want you to know why I felt it was necessary to kill myself. To end my life. To end all our lives. All of them.

Okay. Let us get one thing out in the open. After I finish these letters, I'm going to kill myself. Because I know I won't be around when anyone finds my body, I am not living these final moments with the burden of fear. I don't care about exposing my secrets and being honest for once. So that's what I'm going to do. I'm going to be honest about every part of my life. If we're going to die, we may as well die as ourselves. As Rochelle Bampi. No longer afraid of the judgment that will come with what I'm about to tell you, I can begin to kill us, and I want you to know everything about each one of me that I killed today.

Acknowledgement

It took a very long time for me to complete this body of work. I could not have accomplished such a daunting task if I didn't have the support of my dearest friends. I want to thank you for seeing the best in me when I couldn't see it in myself and for not unfriending me! There would have not been a happy ending to my story, had we never crossed paths. For this I am forever grateful. As you'll read here, they not only showed me where to go but they drew me a map and held my hand as we went together. #HomeGirl4Life

-alicia nicole

I

Where Do Black Girls Go To Cry?

There aren't maps that guide you to this place. Where you are free to lay one's burdens down. To cast away doubts or fears. To find strength in your own tears. Where the world does not exist and there is no such thing as time. No judgement. Where coming as you are is fine. Where the roles of mother, daughter, sister and lover, are second to the being that lives within. There are no preconceived notions based on the color of your skin. All that's needed is you, and the drive to inevitably win.

A Son's Mother

Tears were streaming out of the corners of his eyes. Roan was no longer able to hold back the flood of sadness that was bursting from his beautiful brown face. They glided down his chin, the tears, as he stood in the middle of the driveway, screaming. I yelled to get his attention; "Roan," I shouted, "get in the car," I told him. He looked up at me, with his mouth wide open and a look on his face that would hurt any mother's soul, but no words came out. I turned away from him, quickly, walking through the raised garage door, I reached for the box of toys that my father had just thrown out of the house and into the garage, for me to collect.

I knew that Roan hadn't moved a muscle behind me, but I didn't have time to yell at him again. I needed to get as much of our stuff as possible and as fast as possible, before the worst happened. I lifted the box and made my way back toward the car where Roan was still standing. He had stopped crying, but his face had been stained with the evidence of his emotions and his exhaustion was clearly visible.

I placed the box into the back seat of my small, four-door sedan, shoving it all the way over to the passenger side. I turned to grab Roan, shielding my eyes from the blinding sun. I bent over to pick him up as he slumped his body into my arms. "It's okay, mommy got you. Let's get you buckled in," I told him as I placed him in the seat.

"What's happening?" he asked. Although only 6 years old, he was very quick to try to understand situations. It was just the two of us, so we always had to figure things out together. I wasn't that young, older than 29, younger than 35, but I was still making stupid and young mistakes. I didn't know what to tell him. This time it was different.

I paused for a moment. After a few deep breaths and an internal prayer, I said, "Roan, we're leaving and we're going to find some other place to live."

As I slammed the car door, I shifted my eyes away from him and back to the doorway inside the garage, that led to the main foyer, inside the house, where I could plainly see a shadow of a man standing there. Solid. As I walked closer to the garage entrance, I saw him reach for something behind the door. When I reached him, my father, he was holding Roan's suitcase. He shook his head. "You need to get it together Chelle. I don't know who you think you are, coming into my house and talking to me like I'm your child." he said.

I just stared at him. I was over listening to anything he had to say. A man I'd idolized my entire life. I didn't care anymore about what I said or how I said it. I lashed out at him; "I'm tired of you and mom always having something to say. No matter what I do it will always be wrong in your eyes. I never wanted to come back here in the first place." I told him.

I could see the anger and rage begin to swell up inside him. He was a handsome man. He carried himself like someone who demanded respect. In this moment, I could offer none.

"You need to leave Roan here and go and get yourself together. Go check yourself into a crazy house." he said. He was still holding the suitcase in his hand while standing in the doorway. His striped, silk pajama pants dangling over his sandals and his spotless white t-shirt were his everyday attire and today was no different.

"You left food in the basement when I asked you not to even eat down there because of how nasty you were the last time you stayed here." he said, with his nose turned up and chest poked out. "You can't follow directions," he said, "you can't keep a job. You can't even pay your rent. How are you supposed to take care of my grandson?"

Frustrated by his line of questioning, I dug the soles of my boots into the cement, placed my hand on the tool shelf hanging on the wall, and rolled my eyes.

"Do you know what it's like to raise a kid alone?" I asked him. "Do you know what it's like to fail at everything you do and no matter what you do, you can't catch a break?" I continued. "I'm not doing well right now and the last thing I needed was to come and be met at the door by my father, angry because I left a burger in a bag, downstairs, on the bed I was sleeping on, all because I figured I'd eat the rest later. And now instead of me being able to come in, relax, get my thoughts together, I have to take me and my son to a shelter just to find some peace." I fired back.

I could tell by the smirk on his face that he could care less about what I was saying. He interrupted my final plea; "You're dumb as hell if you take your child to a shelter." he said. "Just dumb as hell. Take this suitcase and get out of my garage before I slap the shit out of you. You better watch who you talking to." he finished.

Before he could hand over the suitcase, I began to walk toward him. It was as if my body was being pulled by an invisible force. I spread my fingers and closed my fist, forming a claw shape with my hands. I stopped and stood there, in front of him, with my arms dangling at my sides but my fingers still frozen in that claw like position. I looked at him. I forgot that this man was my father. A man who has cared for me all my life. It no longer mattered. I opened my mouth and out it came.

"I don't give a damn who you are," I said with the bass in my voice now stronger, "just because you are my parents does not give you the right to treat me the way you do. We came here for sanctuary and support but all we received was judgement and criticism. Fuck you." I reached for the suitcase with my arm stretched. He hesitated for a moment, looked at the car, then back at me. He placed the suitcase right outside the door and closed it. I could hear the sound made by the lock, as I grabbed the suitcase handle, walked back to the car, and hurriedly opened the car door.

I threw the suitcase into the passenger seat and closed the door, "Roan are you alright?" I asked. I could see him through the rear-view mirror, but he wouldn't look at me. He muttered a soft, "Yes," and continued to gaze out of the window. I backed out of the driveway and onto the street. I could see the neighbors, coming from their cookie cutter homes, walking toward my parent's house, most likely to see what all the noise was, I thought. I pulled up to the stop sign and made a right.

I paused. I had nowhere to go. I decided we would drive in any direction, so I made a left and continued. My thoughts were racing as I drove. Did that just happen? I thought to myself. My hands were drenched in sweat and shaking. I could barely keep the steering wheel steady. As I drove, my vision became more and more blurry, to the point where I could no longer see the road ahead.

"Baby, we're gonna park for a second." I told Roan. We pulled into a small parking lot behind a 7-11. It was still early in the day and most people were still at work, so there weren't a lot of cars around. There were a few shops in the lot, but they didn't appear to be doing much business. Since my parents moved to this area back in 2004, I never really had the chance to familiarize myself with the local shops. This was the perfect spot for me to pull into, one of the only locations low in traffic where I could take a moment to re-focus.

We parked the over-packed car and I got out. I leaned over and removed a cigarette from the armrest. I was hoping that Roan didn't notice. I turned on the radio and asked him to, "chill out for a sec, I'll be right back. I just have to make a few calls." I said.

To which he replied, "okay."

I sat directly in front of the car, out of sight of Roan, on the hot curb. I lit my cigarette and took a puff. I knew I had to think of something fast. I called around to a few shelters. Each one had a waiting list or was in a location too far for us to drive. I was almost on E and I had no money. My options were slim. I could either call a family member that I don't talk to or try to get to a shelter. I couldn't fathom taking my son to a ghetto shelter and out here in the burbs you never know what you're walking into. People can be racist or abusive when you're vulnerable and I didn't want to take that chance.

I ashed my cigarette. With no other options and no one to talk to, I made my decision. I checked on Roan to make sure he was doing alright. He was. I grabbed a sheet of paper from my briefcase and told him, "I'm just right outside the car babe. If you need anything, let me know." Still shaken from the situation with my father, Roan and I both desperately deserved a break. I was ready for mine. I wrote a few words, folded the paper, and slid it into my back pocket.

We were heading back toward the house now. I pretended as if everything was going to be fine. I pushed play on The Brandy cd and let the music blast through the speakers. Normally, Roan and I would soulfully belt out every song that came on, taking turns singing our favorite lines in "The Boy Is Mine," but this time, we rode in silence. We were only a few minutes away from the house when I pulled over and told Roan, "We need to talk. Let's take a little walk." I said.

We both got out of the car. I put my arm around him and pulled him in closely, as we walked down the street. It was strangely warm for this time of year. Any suburb near Chicago is usually freezing in March but we were both walking without coats and we were warm. It was his spring break, but he never made a big deal out of days like that. We hadn't made any plans before all this happened, but I apologized to him anyway, for his vacation turning out like this. I stopped walking. We were standing on the sidewalk, in the middle of the block. In front of each home stood a perfectly planted tree with perfectly manicured lawns and little to no debris anywhere in site. I realized, looking at all the perfect houses, occupied by their perfect families, this is what Roan deserved. He didn't deserve some shelter and he didn't deserve a mother that couldn't provide for him.

Roan turned and looked at me. I reached down into my back pocket and pulled out the note and handed it to him. "Read it," I said. He opened the folded notebook paper and read each word to himself, silently. He lowered his arms as his body went limp, threw his head back and let out a loud cry.

"You are strong enough mommy, you are strong." he whimpered between each syllable.

He forced his face into my stomach, wrapping his arms around my waist. I got down on my knees and held him in my arms. "Listen, look at me." I said. "What are you?" I asked. To which he replied, "A Bampi." "And what are Bampis?" I asked him. "Strong." he answered. "And what do we do?" I inquired. He responded; "Keep it moving!" "And what else are you?" I asked. "A melaninated king." he recited each answer from memory. "So, let me see you be a Strong king." I told him.

He straightened his back and shook his head, letting me know that he understood. "Ro," I said, "you're going to stay with grandma and granddad for a while. They will take care of you. I promise. No matter what, do not let anything they do or say, change you. You are perfect the way you are." I told him. "Remember none of this is your fault. I just need you to be in a stable home right now." I said. I could tell that he wanted me to change my mind, but I couldn't. It had to be this way. We returned to the car and made our way back to my parent's house.

I lowered the volume and pulled into the driveway slowly. We both exited the car at the same time. The sound of the wind and the leaves dancing was all I could hear. My mind was blank. I grabbed Roan's hand and we made our way past the garage, up the walkway, and to the front door. I hugged Roan tightly, gave him a kiss on his cheek, told him I loved him, and rang the bell. I didn't stand there to wait for someone to answer the door. I ran to the car, jumped in, backed out of the driveway, and sat in the middle of the street until my father appeared in the doorway.

As soon as he opened the door, I sped off down the street and turned the corner. Although time was still ticking, my circumstances had not changed. I was still broke, low on gas with nowhere to go and no one to call. My only thought was, drive into oncoming traffic.

I drove to a nearby outlet mall and parked to gather my thoughts. As I took inventory on the junk spilling over in my car, I began to separate Roan's belongings from my own with the intent to drop them off to him later. There were many of my own belongings inside the car too. I was still in the process of moving things from the apartment we'd just left. *I would be alright if I had to sleep in the car because there was a blanket and pillow,* I thought.

There were a few electronic items and pieces of jewelry I could pawn and that gave me some peace of mind. I sat there in that parking lot for hours. The sun beamed down and there was no escape. I began to remove layers of clothing and I removed my shoes. I parked further enough away from customers and their vehicles but not so far that a police officer would find my loitering, suspicious. I sat there thinking, going over, in my head, how I ended up here.

After darkness fell, I put all my layers of clothing back on. It may have felt like summer in spring during the day but by nighttime, it felt like winter again. I drove back to the house and parked outside. All I wanted was to be close to Roan. I settled into my car for the night, writing, clearing my head and getting my thoughts out. I was still trying to hold on to some type of reality. I knew I had failed him. I just didn't know to what extent and as usual, what to do next.

* * *

Beautiful Trees

Even trees dance when its windy.
There's less fear in the wind.
Subtle gusts provide wings for leaves.
Promises of children's' laughter carried to listening mothers are in the wind.
Branches on trees bow to queens as they pass on windy days.
Leaves wave a slow motioned goodbye as the wind dissipates.
The wind's final roar signals it's pending retreat.
The rhythmic motion of the tree escalates into song and dance when met be wind. Beautiful trees dance to goodbye songs written by the wind. We get caught in the rhythm of life but we forget to dance. Be the tree.

K-Town Girls "a reflection"

I was forced to face how I ended up here because I can look back over my life and say, as a kid, I didn't have any "real" problems. Born on the west side of Chicago, in K-town, our family lived in a small apartment, on the first floor of a three-story building. The building was owned by my mother's teacher's sister who was also, my grandmother's boyfriend's sister. Our families were connected on so many levels. It was like God came down herself and placed all the pieces perfectly so that no matter which direction our free will took us, we'd meet at the perfect moment.

We weren't rich but if we were poor, I had no clue. My mother and father, Karen and Roy, met when they were in high school. The story goes, he really wanted her, but she didn't too much care for him. Chicago born and raised, my father, Roy Sr.,was a force to be reckoned with. He grew up on the streets, bouncing from his mother's home to park benches for sleep at age 7. He sold candy in the parks for extra cash. This man was born a hustler. His mother, young and single, was not in the best of situations to care for him. She drank to numb the pain of her circumstances with 6 boys, and several different fathers.

Back then you were either in a gang or a singing group. My dad was in a singing group. He was the family songbird and when he and his brothers got together, family picnics were like the barbecue scene at the ending of the movie, "The Five Heartbeats." Young and talented, Roy, was charismatic.

With a personality to emulate, Michael Jackson in his boyhood. He lit up any room he entered. He would attend a neighborhood church with some of his brothers and the boys in his singing group when he got older. Attending the local high school and doing God knows what, he bumped into a little skinny girl with two faux Afro puffs who also attended the same church.

Karen, born and raised in Chicago, was Roy's opposite in every way possible. She came from a two-parent household. Her parents from the south, were traditional, married young, and had greatly migrated to find work in the Midwest. They lived a middle-class life with their six kids. Three girls and three boys.

My mother was shy. She spent most of her time at church, working and with her few friends. Her hair was her biggest frustration at times. Once, while walking down the school hallway, a boy grabbed her Afro puffs from her head and went running down the hallway screaming "I got the puff, I got the puff." This made my mom very withdrawn. Somehow, she and my father ended up together and were married at the age of 20 and 21.

My mother worked all the time. She worked as an office assistant most of my life. My father was ex-military and would work where he could find a job before he settled into his position as a postal worker. He was a musician and enjoyed performing in his youth. He's a natural born entertainer if you ask me. My parents lived a humble life. We didn't have everything, but we had what we needed. If they struggled, we didn't know about it. I was the middle child. My parents also had my older brother and my younger sister. This was our family. Somehow my parents made it work.

The west side of Chicago was every bit of Crooklyn, the movie. On a hot summer's day, you could easily spot 4 or 5 little girls all spread out on opposite sides of the street. Each one jumping rope or playing with her Skip-it, protected between two light posts, this was our designated playing area. The snowball lady would sit out front with her cane draped across the railing. Sitting next to her, an ice chest filled with ice she would shave into a Styrofoam cup and she would cover it with flavored syrup. I'd get several flavors in one snow-cone, let it melt a little, turn it upside down in the cup and suck out all the juice.

Before my sister was born, my mom found babysitters through friends or parents at the school. However, she found them, it wasn't your modern-day, online nanny service. They were usually just okay. I had an attitude problem, so I wasn't going to like them anyway. I hated people telling me what to do, even at the age of 6. My brother and I began going to a babysitter who had 3 children of her own. The youngest, a year and a half older than me, was in the same class as my brother. She was pretty and at the time, I thought she was nice.

When it first happened, I was in first grade at a catholic school. We wore yellow and green plaid jumpers and I'm sure I had a head full of braids with beads on them. The kind that make noise when you jump up and down. Sometimes my mother would put bows in my hair, but I didn't like them because they didn't make enough noise. I don't know how it started. I just remember lying on her mother's bathroom floor with the sink standing over me, as I held on to its silver legs. With my plaid jumper-dress ruffled in between me and her, she was touching me in a way I had never been touched before. Kissing my lips, I felt the warm wetness of her tongue glide over mine. I don't know why I opened my mouth, but I did. She humped my leg. She kissed me. She touched me and made me touch her. I don't know what went through my head. I kept my eyes glued to the top of the white sink with its dirty pipes. I don't know what I was supposed to be feeling, if this is wrong, if this is right?

Now that I think about it, I realize, someone did this to her too. I saw her in the hallway going to class a few days later, after the first incident, maybe it was the very next day. She was in her class line walking into her classroom and I was in my class line preparing to walk into my classroom next door. I waved at her and my brother. They were after all, in the same class. She giggled, placed her hand over her mouth, and whispered something to her classmates. Thinking she didn't notice me, I called her name, smiled and waved. She looked right at me and yelled out, "she's gay". I died a little at that moment. I was so young and so trusting. And what is gay? This went on for a little time. I began to act out in school and wet myself. I began to do this very same thing she did to me, to others. I did it to family, friends, neighbors. Anyone who would let me. Just as I had allowed her to.

I held on to my anger for years. I'm only letting it go now because I have no choice. I never really cried over that. I don't know if I was more hurt because this was done to me, that I was humiliated, or that I allowed this to happen and even became the molester myself.

As time went on and I got older, my mother would get clothing made by her mother and I would have to go and get fitted and stand there and pretend as if, even after ten years, I wasn't still pissed. I blamed her for showing me this and making me think it was alright to do these things to others. This was the first time I really had my own problems that involved no one else. This was the first time I had to decide what was wrong or right and I couldn't. I didn't. I didn't grow out of this phase until I was in 7th grade. I should have cried over this a long time ago. I wish I would have cried. I didn't know where I could go to cry. No one ever told me it was okay to come talk to them with my problems.

I guess they assumed I didn't have any because I was so young. That's one amenity my village didn't offer, a place for girls like me to openly cry. As time moved on and I got a little older, I struggled with expressing myself. No longer the little carefree girl that knew all the answers to every question, I began to hold grudges and to put my anger on display for anyone to see. I lost all control I thought I had, and I ran from any confrontation.

* * *

When I was in the second grade, my teacher's name was Mrs. Katrel. She was young, high yellow and pretty. She had hair like you see on a wig, but it looked pretty on her.

"Does everyone have their homework before we go to the science fair," she asked the class. I knew that I didn't have my homework because I never did it. I didn't even understand the meaning behind taking a worksheet home to follow the directions and write my name on the top. It's a waste of my time and I'm not doing it. Plus, I forgot to do it. I passed up an old piece of paper from one of our old assignments. I figured she wouldn't check the papers until later anyway since we had a science fair to get to.

Mrs. Katrel collected the papers from each row. I stared at my desk noticing the missing screw on the inside of the desk opening, where I kept my workbooks and pencils. She walked the room slowly checking each paper and each name. I knew I was about to be in a world of trouble. I could feel her eyes on the back of my neck.

"Rochelle Bampi," I heard her say my name, but I hesitated to look at her. Standing over me, she asks me where my homework was. She knew I didn't do my homework; all of this was just for show. Cue in my attitude! I was going to tell her anything I could to get her away from me. "I left it at home," I told her. "Then why did you pass this old assignment up," she asked. I stumbled on my words. I wasn't prepared for her line of questioning. I didn't know what to say. I could tell that she was very angry. I waited for her to walk away and for the confrontation to be over, but she only got closer to me. I felt the lifting of the back of my shirt before I knew what happened. She had balled the old homework assignment into a crumpled piece of paper now.

Without hesitation, Mrs. Katrel took the crumpled piece of paper and stuck it down the back of my shirt and walked away. I sat there, mad as hell, embarrassed, hurt, in a class of my peers where no learning occurred. I was too young for this to break me down. I realized then that I was sensitive. Not only was I emotional but I had to deal with being damn near empathetic. This would come in handy later in life when I began to blend in more or try to.

A few months after the incident, one of my classmate's mother, molly whopped Mrs. Katrel in the school main office for how she talked to her daughter. Sometimes I wished I had a mother who was about that life, who would believe me, defend me, and love me the way her mother displayed her love for her daughter. My relationship with my mother suffered the most. I blamed her for everything that I had become. I cast all my inadequacies onto her as her sole responsibility.

* * *

It was field-trip day in 5th grade and I was beaming on this morning, realizing I'm going to get to go on a trip with my classmates this time and I usually miss out on everything. I was low key excited. I wanted to stop at the store to get some snacks for my lunch. One of the best parts of a field trip, is not eating school lunch and seeing what snacks everyone has. You know, the usual. Some flaming hot Cheetos, a quarter water, and some Twinkies. My mom said something about not having time and we're going to be late so we couldn't stop. I don't really remember the reason why; all I know is I was mad. I didn't talk to her the whole ride to school.

When I got to school, I jumped out the van and slammed the door. I didn't say goodbye to her. I walked into the class and didn't even say hello to Mrs. Robinson. We called her the peanut lady because she was infatuated with Dr. George Carver and could tell you any arbitrary Black history fact. She was my favorite teacher and I had the most respect for her. Our 5th grade class hung on her every word. She was one of the original rapping Black teachers.

My butt couldn't hit the seat fast enough before I heard footsteps and saw Mrs. Robinson frown her face up and put her hands out as if to hold someone back from beating the mess out of someone. I lifted my head to look towards the door without anyone noticing I was looking in that direction. I knew in the back of my mind, but I needed confirmation.

Who do I see come around the corner? My mama. She was not smiling, not laughing, she looked like she was beyond pissed off. She tried to yell for me saying, "Chelle, come here." By this time, I'm looking at the class like I don't know whose crazy mother this is disturbing our classroom, how rude!

Mrs. Robinson was staring at me and all I could see was that big Dr. Carver peanut dangling around her neck. I asked her in a low voice, "who me" while pointing to myself. She motioned for me to return to the door entrance. By this time, I'm walking as slow as a turtle, counting my steps before I reach the threshold and the ass-whooping I'm about to receive in front of all the kids I hated but want to look cool in front of.

I barely turn into the hallway before I hear my mama utter the words, "do we have a problem?" I knew better. I knew better than to test this crazy lady when we were out in public. She could cut you down to size with a glance and a mumbled word. Loud or quiet, I always knew exactly what she was trying to say, and her point always came across clearly.

I rolled my eyes and snapped back replying with much attitude in my voice, a tilted head, and absolutely no eye contact, "naw." She reached around and slapped me into next week. I mean I really think I saw the future. I was caught off guard. I had tested her before, and she was always able to keep her composure while out in public, so I just knew *all* she was going to do was yell at me. I could handle a little yelling.

With little to no warning, her hand landed on my face and sent chills up my body. I was pissed. Students and faculty members began searching for the commotion. Since we were standing in the hallway, we were easy to locate. I fought back the tears as I felt myself begin to swell with anger. She ushered me back to the van parked outside in front of the school building.

I don't even understand why we're doing all of this, I thought to myself.

Each footstep feels heavier than the last. I get in the van, in the back of course because I'm angry and I don't want to sit next to her. By this time, I'm in the back seat rolling my eyes and making noises with my mouth to show how upset I am. As soon as my mom realizes I'm intentionally not sitting near her and I still have an attitude, she is taken over by complete frustration and rage.

She slams her driver door and comes all the way around to the backseat passenger side. I tossed her a glance that told all too easily how I was really feeling. She jumped at me, grabbed the lunchbox lying on the floor of the minivan and began to hit me with it. I started to fight back and tried to defend myself. This only made things worse. The more I struggled the angrier she became. She reached for the umbrella, on account that it was raining that day. I'm trying to dodge her lashes but I'm skinny and not prepared for this on any type of level. I heard a faint knock on the van door. It was open but only partially.

I heard Mrs. Robinson say, "You need to do that at home."

If you think I'm going to take a ride to my own beat down by assailant, you crazy as hell, I thought to myself. I started to plan my escape. It wasn't long before we were turning down our block. The van door flew open. I felt this empty butterfly feeling fly all through my body again. I was standing out on the pavement before my mom could shift into park.

It was slightly chilly outside but warm enough that I didn't need a jacket. I slammed the door shut and took off running up the street. It wasn't like I was fast or anything, I think I just caught her off guard because she didn't move for a few seconds after she saw me running.

So I'm running, running away from this whooping I know I'm bound to get no matter what but the way my mama just beat my ass in the backseat of that minivan in front of my 5th grade class was the worst thing that could've happened in my life. I had no clue why I was running for real, but something in me said fight or flight, so I chose the latter.

Between hurried asthmatic breaths and weak short strides I think I can hear my mom scream my name. So now I'm running and thinking, two things I should refrain from ever trying to do after today. I crossed the street. We lived on the west side of Chicago which means I wouldn't normally cross the street without a grown up around, but my life is on the line, so I had to do what I had to do. As I'm crossing the street and trying to look back to see if my crazy mama is about to run up on me or if she's going to run up over me with the van, either way, I was trying to be prepared, so as I cross the street I'm trying to figure out how the heck did we end up here.

Like, what went wrong today?

I'm crossing the street and the gang way at the same time, diagonally. I'm moving quickly but I can hear a faint splash to my left side. I can hear someone make a splash in the puddles of water leftover from the rain that occurred earlier in the morning. A quick glance and I am staring right in the face of a dirty dingy dog. He looked like one of those dogs from the neighborhood that has rabies. The dog wasn't really paying me any attention, but I was giving him all the attention in the world. I don't know what happened, but something said, "run Chelle".

I made it across the street and the gangway simultaneously. I bent down and picked up a stick that was lying around just in case the stray dog with rabies tried to attack me. Focusing now back on to the running, and no longer being sized up for the dog's dinner, I was contemplating my getaway plan. I started thinking of places to go. I only knew one person that stayed on this block and she didn't live far from where I was standing.

With my stick in hand, I ran towards Patrice's house. I ran up the steps of her building and rang every bell. My thoughts shifted to practicing my explanation. Who would I say I was running from? How would I explain myself for running away? My thoughts were abruptly interrupted by the inner swing of the heavy wood framed door that was standing in front of me.

"Baby who you looking for," I heard the voice of the little old woman standing in front of me in her nightgown and cornrowed grey hair. I couldn't get out a word. I stood there looking up at her and tightly gripping my stick. I blurted out my friend's name, "Patrice" I said with urgency. "'Trice is at school," she said while her eyes danced from my feet to my head. I completely forgot that it was still morning, and everyone was in school. "Where your mama?" she asked with her words echoing from each home, repeated by each mother in our small but protective village.

Realizing that I was in shock and couldn't get out many words, she handed me the phone. I wrapped the cord around my hand to keep from tripping over it. I dialed numbers that I knew would lead to nowhere to give me more time to figure this situation out. I heard tires come to a screeching halt and doors slammed. I knew it was all over for me, but I refused to go down without fighting for my rights first.

She stood in front of me, Karen, begging me, pleading me to put the stick down and come with her. Looking down at my hand, I had forgotten all about this stick. I couldn't let it go now. "Put the stick down" my mom yelled. How do I explain that I got this stick to fight off the stray dog with rabies? I can't so I just need to tell her how I feel. Here goes.

"Come on Chelle", I heard my father's voice as he approached the porch steps. My mother had called him from the old lady's house phone while I pleaded for my life in monologues and rebuked accusations.

"Come get your daughter," I overheard her say. Now I'm really in trouble. If you wake my father up during his nap, you're just asking to get a whooping. His approach was much different from my mothers, he swooped in like a savior to us both. His demeanor was always cool. "Come on Chelle," he repeated as he held out for me to take his hand. He didn't yell. I walked down the stairs, towards his outstretched hand. As my mother rolled her eyes and returned to the Bampi family van, my father and I began to walk in the direction of our apartment and back on to our block.

He placed his arm around me as we walked to the apartment. "What were you going to do with that stick," he asked jokingly as he removed it from my hands and tossed it aside. "It was for the dog," I replied. "What dog Chelle?" "There was a big dog with rabies chasing me," I explained. He laughed and replied, "well you know your mom thinks you were going to use it on her?"

How could she think I was going to hurt her, I wondered? She was the one beating my butt in the back of a van, in front of my entire fifth grade class. I had no sympathy for her or for her confused interpretations of the situation. After a short five-minute walk, we were home. Immediately, I was sent to the room I shared with my brother.

Dark and quiet because both my siblings were at school, I cried my way into the bedroom and melted into the separated, twin, bunk-bed. I only sat there for a few moments before I heard, "Chelle, come here." As I approached the kitchen parallel to my bedroom, only separated by a door, I was caught off guard. They were both standing there, both of my parents, standing together. My mother stood nearest the chair. My father guarding her by wedging her between he and this chair was holding "the belt". My brother named it that way. We would wager on who could take a whooping the longest without crying. I usually won.

It was leather and thick. We didn't get whoopings often but when we did, it was horrible. My mom sat in the chair first. She motioned for me to lay across her lap, face-down. She and my father took turns whooping my ass. I danced all around that kitchen trying to run. I knew the only reason this went so far was because my mother was embarrassed. All I was doing was normal fight or flight behavior. I have no clue what they expected of me.

I may be a kid but I'm still human and unfortunately tapping into so many thoughts that I can barely function. I wanted to tell them, after this night of course, that I was sorry. Something told me that I should explain myself.

I tried to but my cries of surrender fell on deaf ears. I stopped expressing myself as much, after this happened. It was easier to just go with the flow and try not to show true emotion. True emotion is threatening and if someone doesn't like the way you showed your emotion, there will inevitably provide an opportunity for undesirable confrontation.

I lived out the remainder of my fifth-grade year mostly doing the dishes because I stayed on punishment. The most they'd let me do is go to church and choir rehearsal. My attitude got worse. The more people tried to shape me and parent me, the more I rebelled. My mom was not the "company" type. If I asked her to have company over to the apartment, 10 out of 10 times, she was going to say no. I didn't have friends. I played with a few girls on the block. Patrice was my closest friend until she moved and left me with the third to our trio. Our mothers only allowed us to play with one another when someone was on the porch from either house, to watch us cross the street. I had very few significant friendships. We'd lived on the first floor of the building the Markham's owned all my life.

* * *

Her Name was Miss Markham. I called her Mark or Mama Mark. She was much more than a landlord. To say she was the best woman I'll ever know, wouldn't be saying enough. She was very soft, but you could see the strength in her eyes. She was certain of who she was. She was beautiful. Humble. God loving and fearing. If you saw Mama Mark, you saw her purse, her low heels, and her bible too. She made ice-cream on the back patio. She would let me lick the mixer. She wore these nightgowns that put Tyler Perry's Madea to shame. I watched her closely. I never really understood what was going on when one of the kids off the block came to visit her.

He had his ceremonial gown for his high school graduation or college I don't know. Anyway, he was so excited to share with Mama Mark his graduation news and they were both just beaming, smiling from ear to ear. She was sincerely happy for him and proud of him and I could tell. He told her how much it meant to him that she was proud of him and I believed him.

I was young and couldn't really understand the exchange and plus, I know I'm not supposed to be in grown folk business when they are talking, but I was still somehow affected by it.

I wanted to have that connection with someone, and I wanted to command that type of respect. I think because of how much I truly already valued her, I enjoyed seeing others value her as well. Mama Mark was there for my parents during the infancy of their marriage. Her and her husband, Mr. Mark. I loved him too. He was a strict, "stay off the grass, I sleep with a shotgun under my bed" type of man. I remember one time I got beat up on the school bus coming home from school. Mr. Mark fixed me up, made me a bologna sandwich, and gave me a very stern talking to about letting people put their hands on me. The next day, he was standing on the corner waiting for the bus to arrive. He made sure no one beat me up that day. He unknowingly taught me the lesson that, when people go to battle for you, you go to war for them.

There is nothing I wouldn't have done for these two. They were my first taste of happiness outside of my immediate family. I had no expectations of them, and they didn't disappoint. Not without flaws, Mississippi bread, these two represented something that I'm only now beginning to understand. I thought all people were like the people in my building. We were a family. Their daughter became my Godmother over time. We share a wonderful bond. For the first time in my life I saw someone's pure soul and it was beautiful. I wondered, was every human the same way? I experienced pure joy and it was amazing. I found out early on how wrong I was to think everyone would be like the Markham's.

Dream Endlessly

It was two days later. The morning immediately following the argument with my father, I left before anyone could see me. I pawned a few items and used my hotel points for a complimentary one-night stay and dinner. During all the commotion, I had forgotten that I had made a commitment to one of my longtime friends. I gathered my belongings and packed them neatly into my car. I had rearranged everything inside, so it didn't seem as if I was living out of my car, although I was. I took the last bit of money left over from the television I pawned and gassed up the old Cobalt. I was already running late to the city, but I told the kids I would bring food, so I had to make another stop.

When I arrived, the kids were waiting! They were more than willing to run outside in the rain to grab all the food, plates, and drinks. I said my apologies and we made our way into our designated group area to begin this week's lesson.

"Tears, are capable of breaking, even the strongest girls among us, down," she began reading, "they make us all uncomfortable no matter the situation," she continued slowly, "in ways that are too uncomfortable to even discuss; So we cry alone," she finished.

I could see the tears building in her eyes as she said the words aloud. Her voice slightly higher than a whisper. We all stared at her. Wedged between the cafeteria table with the orange stool pressed into the backs of her legs, grasping the notebook paper with clenched fingers. She balanced herself as she quickly jotted down a few more words onto her essay.

Having completed jotting down her notes, she stood, with her body pressed into the table. I nodded in her direction and caught her glance. She returned the nod, locking eyes with mine. The extra nod and head shake, she gave, let me know that she was okay and could make it through the remainder of our dream session, so I motioned for her to continue reading.

Her voice was shaky and filled with emotion. Soft, yet powerful. Here she was, all of 16 years old, a buck 25 soaking wet, but her words, *her words were much older and made her appear much stronger than she imagined herself.* I thought.

"Hunger pains feel similar to period cramps, ask me how I know." she paused. Looking at her face, it was like she wanted us to hear what she was saying, only, she didn't want to have to say it. I wasn't sure what she would say next, so I walked around the table, slowly, muffling the sound of the heel of my thigh-high, leather boots, with each step taken, trying not to disturb her as she read.

Each seat was filled with a child. Although the group was male dominated, we had emotional moments like this one, very often. I could hear the boys begin to shuffle their feet under the table. One kid let out a heavy sigh. *If I could feel his negative energy, I was sure that she could too,* I thought to myself. "In this space we are all safe to be who we are," I said. "Let's give Alexis the same respect you'd want her to give you, stop shuffling your feet around." I said. The room got quieter. All eyes were looking in my direction now. I knew I had their attention.

"Listen," I said. "Dr. D will kill me if you all do not finish these dream books. Dr. D and I go way back," I told them, "we met in junior high. We weren't best friends or anything, but we shared a mutual respect. We stayed in contact over the years with the help of social media. When she started her Dream Endlessly program, I was overly excited to participate as one of the mentors. We are all adult dreamers sharing our passions with you young dreamers and I am so proud to be among such amazingly, kindhearted individuals. So, let's get this work done y'all." I said with excitement. "Dr. D doesn't play any games and I don't know about y'all but I'm not about that life dream-girls and boys."

They all laughed. Unsure if my mini motivational speech had worked, I scanned the room, looking at each kid, making sure that what was understood, was understood. Beaming with restored confidence, Alexis began to speak again.

"When I was a little younger than I am today, my grandmother would lock the refrigerator with a special padlock to keep me away from the food."

The room became completely quiet as she spoke. The boys paused their conversations and Laticia, the only other girl in the group, turned her head up and stared as Alexis continued.

"She set aside small portions of the nastiest food for me and my brother but when she fixed her plate, she had real people food."

She was reading her words without taking a breath. "We would go to bed hungry and go to school hungry," she said. "My grandmother told me to my face, that she hated me, and I believed her. There were so many times I wanted to cry but felt embarrassed or too ashamed," she said. "That's my worst memory, thank you."

She took her seat as we all looked at one another. The sadness in the air began to swarm around us like a hurricane. "Okay," I said, interrupting the unavoidable silence, "well hell," I said. Unable to find the words to say to the group next, I walked over to where Alexis was sitting. I knelt and took her hands in mine. "Look at me," I said. Biting her lip and holstering her elbows into the sides of her waist, she peeked under her eyelids, shyly, granting my wish.

"You are beautifully and wonderfully made, and I apologize for her, I'm sorry." "Is it okay if I give you a hug?" I asked. She embraced me as I opened my arms. She snuggled underneath them like I was a warm sweater.

"Miss Rochelle," she said, "you smell good, what is that you got on, Riri?" she asked. Laughing, I returned to the head of the table, I confessed that I had no clue what perfume I was wearing, if any, and it certainly wasn't any fancy perfume from some superstar songstress. "I don't follow the trends," I told her as I shot her a quick wink and a smile. "You smell soap boo, soap."

At the head of the table again, I beckoned for everyone's attention. "I want you all to consider this," I said, "you will all have a story to tell one day. Some of you will figure out your story sooner rather than later. It's up to you how you use that story." I told them. "The whole point of this exercise is so that you can realize your worst nightmare, your worst memory, and then you can find the dream in that pain and hurt, then use that to write your dream piece," I said, "It's better for you to channel that pain into passion now more than later."

The seriousness in my voice and my carefully chosen words ensured them that I had firsthand knowledge of this subject. They passed up their assignments one by one. Each one handing their paper to the person seated next to them. "Here you go Miss Rochelle," said Cordell, as he stood to hand me the stack of papers. He was always very helpful. A little shy, he was the smallest in the group. I could tell that he came from a more stable home than most of the kids but for some reason, he tried extra hard to be more hood than he needed to be.

"What's all that writing on your clothes?" I asked him.

"Man, Joe, I mean, Miss Rochelle, you know this that new MUROB LEAHCIM." he said as he grabbed his chin, stepped back, and leaned to the side, providing plenty of room for me to admire his outfit.

"Cordell, you know you got issues right," I laughed.

"Man, I'm just saying miss Rochelle, I know a good joint when I see one." He smirked. "And what makes this guy's clothes so good?" I asked him.

"Well for starters," he answered, "this designer is from the Chi, born and raised. He takes high quality fabrics and combines them with designs that you can tell come straight from our culture," he said with excitement. "Feel this," he said while pointing to his zippered hoodie. "I think this is the softest thing I own," he said.

"Dang boy," I said, interrupting him, "I don't think I've ever seen you so excited to talk about anything before," I told him. He quickly changed his demeanor. I could tell that he didn't like the extra attention. Moving the conversation in another direction as the rest of the group began to talk louder and louder at the table among themselves, I asked him, "did you complete today's assignment because you Know you never finish an assignment," I shot him a look that said, and you know I'm telling the truth.

"Come on Miss Rochelle," he smirked. "Why you always put somebody on blast?" he asked.

"You put yourself on blast when you don't allow yourself the opportunity to be great in all that you do." I told him.

"Miss Rochelle, you always spitting that positive talk," he said while returning to the table.

"As opposed to spitting what?" I asked him. "

You know," speaking louder now and with a deeper voice now that he was back with his boys, he said, "all adults talk about the struggle and pushing to be your best self but in reality, all y'all don't have to go through what we go through," his boys backed him up as he went on, "take you Miss Rochelle, you look like you got it all."

I laughed. "Boy, if you only knew," I said. "We all struggle, we all fall or go through something traumatic that changes us," I was talking to each individual kid now. Gliding from one side of the room to the next, I asked, "what about me makes you think that my life is easy or that you have it harder than me?"

"For number one," Laticia answered, "you talk like a white girl." As soon as the words escaped her lips, I began to feel my face melting into the collar of my turtleneck sweater. Although, I was disgusted by such a remark, this wasn't my first-time hearing this and I was certain that it wouldn't be my last.

"Laticia," I said, "baby girl, there are so many things wrong with that statement that I don't have a clue where to even begin," I told her. "I don't think there is a such thing as talking like a race," I said. "Think about it, Black people are the most diverse race of humans on this planet, we all sound different from one another." Right?" I asked.

"Yeah but some of us Black people sound more like White people than others do." replied Laticia, mockingly.

I could tell that we were going to get off subject, I tried to steer the conversation back to our original question. "So, I get that I sound suburban and educated," I said, sarcastically, "but what does that have to do with you assuming I have it all, assuming that I don't have my own painful story, or that I can't relate to y'all?" I asked. "Sit down and shut up." I told them. "And I'm gone tell you about growing up in the middle-class suburbs outside of Chicago."

We all gathered around the table. We each began to grab a paper plate, a few chicken wings, a handful of fries and we smothered it in mild sauce. As we all found our seat at the table, I began.

* * *

"I was going into the sixth grade when we moved from the city to a suburb called Bolingbrook, IL. At first appearance, as a kid, we had come up, in my mind. But it's when you're that young and the new neighbor's kid's chosen topic of discussion, every time you pass by their front yard, is of how your family was not welcomed there. One of the little girls went as far as to say that they held a meeting about my parents buying that house with them being Black and everything.

I was always on punishment, still had to do the dishes and I still had major attitude issues. We would visit the city from time to time. As the project buildings were being torn down and communities torn apart, my father would organize a family cookout and get each side of our family together. Sometimes he and I would dress up in matching clown suits and we would get the party started. Dancing, playing around with my dad was always a time of enjoyment for me. Away from my daily dishes' duty, I was free. Someone shouted out 'dance contest for the kids' one year. That's when I was pushed from behind. I made my way to the dance line to join in on the competition. I wasn't sure who pushed me, but my innocence figured this would be fun.

This was Chicago in the summertime. Families all at Douglas Park with tents and a grill with loud music and friends. This was what living looked like. Once the music began, I could hear the laughter. It wasn't friendly laughter. I wish I had thicker skin and didn't feel every emotion so strongly.

I had no rhythm and to them, this was funny. Somehow this made me less Black. This was the last time I danced like no one was watching. I never cared to even know if people were watching before this. Now I don't dance, or I dance like others around me.

Life is easier that way. My parents wanted to give us a better chance at succeeding outside the walls of gentrified Chicago. Up until then, the only White people I knew were teachers, doctors, and the people I saw on television. Arriving in this small town of predominantly White people, was a culture shock at first, that turned into a constant state of confusion. Junior high school was rough for me. I didn't have the type of parents that checked my homework for completion, and they were not super involved. They had expectations of their children. They wanted to see a good report card, wanted you to stay out of trouble, and they didn't want to receive any phone calls home from school administration.

I couldn't stay out of trouble to save my own life. I wasn't affiliated with any gang, pretend or not, my parents were still married, and I didn't have any step-siblings, and I spoke my mind. This became the catalyst that led to my every day after school showdown. I ran home from school almost every day. More like I was chased home. This is around the time my brother started smelling himself and found out how much white girls like Black boys in the suburbs. We grew apart and instead of being his bike riding shadow, I became his embarrassing little sister.

I silently faded into the background even more now. Living off in the suburbs can create a wave of lifelong culture shocks. It was there where I learned I was ugly, too dark, and too skinny. I learned I wasn't ghetto enough and not cool enough. Here, I learned that I was a bald-headed-scalawag. I couldn't focus on learning anything the school was trying to teach me. I was too busy working on not being ugly, trying to fit in with my peers, trying to be relevant, trying to survive the ill-mannered children birthed by the good ole suburban folks.

I remember after a language arts class, we were standing in the hallway near the lockers, in between class periods. The new teacher pronounced my name, "Rachel," instead of Rochelle inside of class today. Now I wasn't too upset because Rachel sounded a lot less urban and a lot more refined. So, I went with it. I told the teacher that it was supposed to be pronounced that way. Standing in the middle of our lockers was a little girl who always instigated altercations and ignited situations. If something was wrong with you, she was the first person to tell the world. So, there we were, immediately following class, and although I had forgotten the whole "Rachel" ordeal, she had not. Nor would I after what she said next, for that matter.

"Your name is not Rachel," she said with a level of boldness unmatched by her peers. "Your name is Rochelle," she continued. "You look like a Rochelle. That's a Rachel," she said while pointing to the mixed girl in our locker aisle. And it was true. The mixed girl, with the "good hair", standing in the same locker aisle as we were, the one with the fair skin, it just so happened that her name was also Rachel. You'd think that I was equipped to deal with bullies because we had our fair share of them in the city, but this was a different type of bully.

Our parents were working to keep their suburban homes and to clothe and feed us. We were arguing about who said what to who and which girl was the prettiest. I didn't back down. I always fought back. This made me a target. Being an emotional, sensitive, shit talker doesn't really mix well. I never really messed with anyone but if they messed with me, I didn't turn and hide. My father taught me not to run from bullies. He just forgot to teach me how to fight them.

I tried, for a while, to fit in with the girls who picked on me. These were the pretty Black girls. I always looked at all girls as my sisters. I felt like we were all in this together. But, I was alone. These were not my sisters and they were not the kind of friends you'd want your daughter to hang out with. I really can't recall a time before meeting these little girls where I considered my beauty being something displayed on the outside. I thought if I felt good and treated everyone the way I wanted to be treated, all was beautiful, and I'd be fine. I was wrong.

I had no one to turn to. When you tell your parents that the girls at school hate you and pick on you, they say things like, "just don't hang around them." But they were everywhere. I couldn't get away from them. Being a mean girl was not in my blood. I stayed to myself. My hair was the topic of discussion most days. I dressed like a kid. I was only eleven and I still played with my Babysitter's club dolls. I still talked to my stuffed animals and imagined classrooms on bathroom floor tiles. My hairstyles were either what my mom paid someone to do or what I threw together at the last minute. I never knew how to style my own hair. Never really had a relationship with me in that way. It was never needed.

To these girls, I was bald-headed, and they made sure I knew it. My biggest critic and my bully from sixth to eighth grade had enough hair to wrap around a spaghetti noodle but she had the loudest voice. I lost myself even more during those years. Trying to please everyone around me and being pulled in so many directions with a plethora of clashing priorities. I started being a little less carefree. Did things to make those around me comfortable and dimmed my light more. I wasn't all the way "tapped in" but I was receiving so much information, emotions, and having these mental battles with myself.

My mother would try to help ease my suffering. There wasn't much she could do. She'd stand outside with the dog on his leash and wait for me to walk down the street from school to our house. She thought just by being there, the kids wouldn't tease me. This only made matters worse. Kids can be cruel but not knowing how to cry is even more cruel. A little Black girl has her breaking points. I'm ashamed of myself for feeling sorry for myself. I can hear the voices of women being raped, beaten, and starved, screaming at me telling me to "shut up, what you're going through is nothing. Be strong" so I bottled up my emotions, insecurities, and fears and let them stew.

Life is funny sometimes. You do a lot of laughing during your lifetime, but you also do a lot of crying. Or a lot of holding back your cry for reasons we all know too well. What if you didn't have to hold back your desire to cry? What if there was a place you could go to cry as loud as you wanted to and not one soul would interrupt you?

In the Black family, you have three categories. You have your recently relocated from the projects and first-generation survivalist, second generation survivalist working a 9-5 making ends meet never rising above their class, then you have your black sheep of the second-generation survivalist who knows there is something better out there, a better way to survive. I was the black sheep. I always thought school was bullshit but I loved history and literature. Writing and poetry became my outlet. Although, my mother constantly advised me not to write down all my feelings so often.

It was around this time in my life when I began to keep a diary and take note of the many things happening around me…to me. Most of the pages were filled with boys I thought were cute or requests I made from Dear Diary. On each page I saw a sad and lost little girl. Desperately desiring someone to grant her approval to be herself. There were pages and pages filled with names of boys with hearts and that funny shaped letter "s" that every kid liked to draw. I talked about running away a lot. Talked about going away to college, leaving my mother's control issues, and never looking back. I had it all figured out.

Almost 20 years later I now see where I get this running thing from. I wanted to run from my problems even in high school. My biggest problem being my nagging mother. I don't think life was very kind to my mother. Well, then she had me, so… She grew up in a different time period than me. There were things she couldn't teach her daughters because she had never been taught them herself. She could not prepare me for life after high school or for college because these are experiences, she had never had. I never expected her to have the answers, but I knew that I could figure them out on my own without her direction because her interference would only mess me up.

If I only knew then what I know now. As controlling as she was, I was equally selfish. Always approaching her with an attitude to defend myself from the attitude she would bring. We have never met on an even playing field and we never will. I learned this early, so I tried to do things my way."

The kids were all silent. The food was being tossed in the trash and we had begun our cleanup efforts.

"So that's why you come here Miss Rochelle?" Laticia asked.

"That's part of the reason." I answered. "I come here so that you all can look at me and see someone who truly cares for you and will sacrifice for your success because you deserve it. I didn't have the type of support I needed so I'm offering it to y'all." I told them. "And plus, as much as y'all get on my nerves, you make me a better person."

I was feeling nostalgic being on the west side of Chicago again. I grew up not that far from where the school was. Walking into their school building gave me such a feeling of home. The energy these kids had it was always amazing just to be around them. They were all dealing with something or going through something. Some of their pain came out during our lessons together but what I loved about them is that they were still smiling.

I liked to curse in front of them from time to time. Wanted to let them feel human around me. They were my momentary escape from everything going wrong in my life and I wanted to be theirs. It left a bitter taste in my mouth, packing up my papers to go home. As we wrapped up our session, somehow, the kids talked me into providing the snack for next week. We discussed possible food options for a few minutes before we all decided on chicken with mild sauce, juice, and fries. We would eat and read over our poetry and dream pieces. Everyone was excited. I probably more than they. Living in the suburbs doesn't allow for me to eat some of the best food Chicago has to offer, the food I grew up on, so excited was an understatement but I didn't tell that to the kids.

"I'd rather have pizza," I lied.

"Come on Miss Rochelle," said one of the students.

"Fine," I replied to the group," we can have chicken and mild sauce if you all agree to come prepared to recite your pieces.

I could feel gravity pulling me back down to earth as I walked past the four security guards strategically placed at the school's exit. I was still beaming a little from my time with the kids. I fed off their energy and I hadn't fully come down yet, but I could feel the anxiety building up inside of me as I sat in the car. I was dreading returning to reality. I wanted to stay with the dreamers where I belonged.

A Mother's Daughter

I wrapped the seat belt around my body and grabbed the steering wheel, connected the aux cord into my phone and scrolled down the screen to find the perfect playlist for my long drive home. I could do this drive with my eyes closed. I was in familiar territory, in the hood, my hood, our community. It's amazing how one can find beauty in everything Chicago is. I loved it. With the key in the ignition, I started driving.

I was looking at everything "The Go" had to offer. On that side of town, most faces were Black like mine. You couldn't help but notice stuff like that when you lived in the suburbs. It made you appreciative of seeing reflections of yourself, out in the world. It made you feel connected. Not so much alone. That was important to me. So, I looked at every one of their faces when I drove, and they were beautiful. Chicago was beautiful.

The music playing from my phone was replaced suddenly by the sound of an outdated ringtone that was now blasting from the car speakers. I quickly looked at the phone to see who was calling. I didn't want to take my eyes off the road for longer than I had to. I hated driving without music. It raised my anxiety levels. I don't know why but, for some reason, I was much calmer and more focused when the music was on. I felt like I could do anything.

Looking at the phone, I could see that it was my mother and it was with great reluctance and an abundance of hesitation that I slid my finger down the face of the phone and answered her call.

"Hey", I said. We'd been short with one another since the altercation with my father. She was more like a parole officer than a mother. I knew she could feel my disdain. As much as I despised her, I needed her. I kept trying, with everything in me, to push her away. To not be like her. At some point, I began to loathe all that she was. My mother, Karen, she was an amazing Black woman and I made her life, while raising me, a living hell. It took me years to really understand what a horrible daughter I was. She'd never say it, but I know there were times when she wished she'd never given birth to me. That's OK. I'm completely fine with that because there were times when I wished she'd never given birth to me too.

During my high-school years, we had our share of fights. She and I. Back then, I was clueless, self-centered, co-dependent, and spoiled. My world was the only one I saw. Everything was about me, me, and more me. Every word of guidance she tried to give me went in one ear and out the other. Selfish. Lazy. That is who I was. This is what she told me.

I never saw it though. It's funny how you can live inside your own head for so long and never even know yourself. It's childish and at some point, you must choose to move away from childish things, take responsibility for your life, your actions, your own energy, and the decisions you make.

This is what she taught me, my mother. I don't think she knows what she did for me. How she was still raising me, even well into my thirties. I was her child and she was my mother. For this, I loved her. The turning point in our relationship came suddenly. Neither of us were prepared for what was about to happen. This would be the test. We were embarking on a journey that would prove difficult to endure.

Just the sound of her voice alone, pissed me off. She didn't even need to be saying anything. It just pissed me off. It always did and it probably always will. Sometimes I tried to sound oblivious to the tone in her voice when she spoke to me because she was, after all, my mother and I had learned not to talk back to her. Talking back to her, even though I was grown, was a sure way to have to deal with her intimidating ass attitude for the next few days and I wasn't about that life.

I lived with her. I had to see her every single day and I knew better than to pick a fight with her. Ten times out of ten, she's guaranteed to come out the winner. So, I don't even try anymore. I just try to walk my line and keep the peace.

My overly sensitive nature was tugging at the steering wheel again, but I was determined not to let anything get to me.

"Where are you Chelle," she demanded, dropping the first two letters of my name, as she often did. I wondered if she even remembered my name was Rochelle and not Chelle? "I'm on my way back, driving on 90 right now," I answered. I held on tight to my nerves. I made every attempt I could not to release the heavy sigh that was stirring in my soul, that desperately needed to be released if I was going to hold on to any amount of peace.

"Why is it taking you so long? Did you get paid for doing this? I just don't understand how you can drive all the way to the city to volunteer but you can't get a job," she said. Her words cut like dirty knives, cascading across opened wounds, and the pain was always long-lasting. I was in a very negative headspace. I didn't know how to tell her that I had lost control of my life and that I needed her help, not her judgment. I knew she couldn't understand. Her voice was a reminder of my reality. Of my fears. Of my disappointments. I had now come fully down from the high I was riding. I had become completely disconnected from the energy I had acquired only minutes ago from my precious mentees.

"I'm on my way home," I told her. I could envision her turned up face scowling on the other end of the phone. For over 30 years I've suffered her intimidating, turned-up-faces, and listened to her non-verbal judgment. "Mom," I said, "I am on my way from the city as planned. I finished mentoring and got directly on the road. As I said I would, this morning when I called you to check on Roan. It was nice; I was able to share my passion of storytelling with the kids. They really inspired me," I said, campaigning for my rights long before she'd have a chance to highlight the cons of the situation.

"That's nice Chelle," she said very mockingly. I could tell she didn't really give a damn. She was about to start in on me, I knew it. I was counting down the seconds in my head. She was about to do what she did best. She was about to start lecturing me in a second. She couldn't help herself. When she starts worrying or when something is not the way she has decided it should be, she gets all disoriented and her only resolve is to lecture you.

I got my stubbornness from her. I wondered, if she knew how close to the edge I really was, would she still push me so hard? *You can push your kids away sometimes with all of that pushing,* I thought to myself. I listened to her as she began to tell me about whatever it was that I did today to get on her nerves. As there was always something. She complained about me to me almost daily.

"We can't watch Roan on your schedule, we have jobs Chelle," she said, "real jobs," she added. I wasn't the least bit surprised that she was calling to rush me home to get Roan, but I still found myself reminding her, "I don't ask you to watch him often," I replied." I ask you to watch him once in a blue moon, if that," I explained.

"You need to figure out what you're doing with your life," she proclaimed, as if this was a new concept, she was introducing into my life for the very first time. This was her everyday speech that fell upon my deaf and depressed ears. I could feel my hands begin to drip with perspiration. My arms and back stiffened. My eyes began to fill with tears. I fought every breath to sound normal as I pulled over to the side of the road. I parked and I sat there. In this moment I just wanted to let everything out. To let someone else in. There was so much that I wanted to say but I chose, I decided, to remain quiet. Somehow, I had convinced myself that remaining quiet and not crying was protocol.

There was so much that I could've told my mother. Wish I knew how to tell my mother. Every conversation ends the same with us. I don't even try anymore. Sitting here, listening to all my mother's judgments, I couldn't help but to allow my mind to race off to pinpoint the exact moment that I should have cried but didn't. Why is it so normal for me to safeguard my tears?

* * *

If junior high was the culture shock I never asked for, high school was the lesson I never learned from. In high school, I was determined not to be that kid. This time I would be more involved. There we were, sitting in the freshman volleyball tryouts.

I've never played a sport in my life. Nevertheless, the upperclassmen were casually discussing their after-school sex escapades. I was amazed. I couldn't believe they knew anything about sex, especially that they were doing it. I didn't make the team, but I learned a lot about sex that night.

My brother was just a junior. He was off in his own world of girls and basketball. I could tell, anytime I got near him, he wanted me to disappear. He offered no direction and my parents trusted the flawed school system so there was little to no guidance there either. I took the classes that sounded interesting and whatever the school automatically enrolled me in. I did the bare minimum in class. I had trouble focusing. I never told anyone because I thought it made me seem weak. I was desperately trying to order some Focus Faster from the infomercial.

I was already too much of a loner by Junior year. I had made, what I considered to be, friends; although my father never hesitated to remind me that I didn't have friends, I only had associates.

There were four of us Lemon, Baby Girl, Cookies n' cream and Strawberry. I don't remember how we picked our names, but we used gel ink pens on black paper-lined notebooks, to communicate. We signed our notes, LYLAS (Love You Like a Sister). We did or, at least, we tried. Lemon and I, Baby girl, attended one high school and the other two went to our rival high school. We were all familiar with one another from junior high, but we connected more in our later years.

Each one I admired for different reasons. Lemon, my best friend was opposite to me in every way physically possible. She was the tall, skinny, light skin girl, with huge pretty brown hair, athletic, modelesque figure and she was everything every girl wanted to be and every boy wanted to be with. Everything I wanted to be. By watching them, although be it too late, I learned to indulge in the suburban lifestyle.

We enjoyed ROTC, driver's education, and choir as electives, Rotary club partnerships, theater club, and pageants. Pageants in which I won. My mom was stuck in the days of her own youth. Where the city life, offered a young girl city things not to be found in the suburbs. The concessions made for my comfort were invisible, to say the least. How easy was it for her to forget me, the skinny Black girl who has no idea where she came from or where she was going?

Unlike Chicago in the seventies, where my mother and other mothers were forgoing their adolescents for wedding rings, these suburban streets were not filled with buses to transport an inquisitive mind, community activists to help steer a child, specifically, in these corn-filled lands. There was a gap left unfilled. Possibly one of the best decisions she would make during this period of my life, was to search until she found a church for our family.

This was one of the defining communities in my life. Sophomore year I began to think of what I would do with myself after high school, with all the children in my new community planning their next milestones, I could easily notice the difference between my plan and their plan. There hadn't been one college graduate on either side of my family, so preparation was poor. There was no college fund or matching agreement from my parents. I had a hard time getting my mother's taxes to complete the FAFSA, so looking for additional assistance would prove useless.

Not too many options and an abundance of opinions later, I decided I would do what most Black people who wanted to get out of the community or into college did. I was going to join the military. I was not your typical patriot and I didn't grow up dreaming of protecting anyone, including myself, by killing anyone else. I swallowed my pride for once in my life and contemplated joining the armed forces, for the financial assistance only. Sometimes when given no concrete direction, you'll end up traveling in that direction in which you've seen others go.

High school recruitment of black students into the military was more common to me than college recruitment. My parents were doubtful but relieved when I revealed my plan to join the military. I was even bold enough to carry my ass to MEPS, where the military admission process begins. I took the exam, written and physical. Then I was told, "my asthma would not allow my entrance into any type of armed services." I was slightly disappointed, but the weekend did offer a consolation prize. His name was Timothy, Timmy for short.

* * *

The phone in my hotel rang as I gathered my clothes and toiletries, packing to return home the following morning. After learning that the military didn't want me and preparing to return home a failure, I answered thinking it was my mother calling to check on me. Besides, no one else had the number anyway so it had to be her.

"Hello," I answered. The voice on the other end quickly grabbed my attention. It wasn't my mother nor my recruiter. This was a young man. A boy with nothing else better to do but to ring random phones in the same hotel as he. With my voice well trained for situations such as this from countless hours sitting on the party line, and with boredom setting in, I was game for a prank caller.

We stayed on the phone for a while. He was a city boy, a South-sider, a hood boy, but his conversation was just what I needed. We met in the dining hall after much hesitation on my part. He was cute and made me feel as if there were only two people left in the world, him and I. We vowed to keep in contact and although he got in and I didn't, I promised to support him in his journey. My first real boyfriend. We dated while he was away in basic training and wrote letters to one another. At this age, almost 17 and going into my Junior year in high school, my focus was on finding my husband because that's what I thought you were supposed to do.

Before him, my plan of action to exit my mother's controlling household was the road I was denied access to and I had no plan b. Timmy, had a plan. He was going off to college, an HBCU. My love for him drove me to desire to do the same. I jumped into action, requesting admission packets from every school possible, from Harvard to the random local schools not too far from the suburb in which we lived. I started to research, and this is when I found out that I was not prepared for this part of life at all. I was determined. I knew I had to get the hell out of my mom's house but with no money, no support, and little to no knowledge about the process, I began to dig myself into a hole deeper than anyone could imagine.

After teaching myself all about the college admission process and what it would take for my own entrance into such an establishment, I took on the responsibility of securing my own finances. Accepted into the same HBCU as Timmy, I knew I had to find the money. I won scholarships from my church and from the town rotary club, but it still wasn't enough. I had a job but no car to rely on for extra hours and nowhere else to turn until one day, Lemon, my best friend, showed me an ad in the paper about a local scholarship pageant for juniors. I took the paper home and made the phone call to inquire about the qualifications. Turned out, I was the perfect candidate.

I began the process of registering and attending the meetings for the participants. When I told my mother she protested saying, "you're not prepared for something like this." I knew that I was, so I went ahead anyway. She drove me to look for dresses and arranged for my uncle to drive me to my judges' interview because she was busy. After all my work was done and we had practiced until we couldn't practice any longer, it was time for the competition. The girls, my opponents, were more than prepared for an event such as this. I was out of my league, but I tried not to let it show. We had formed a bond and I was studying them, learning from them, but I doubt that they knew it.

On the day of the competition my family attended and brought my grandparents and Timmy came too. I think it surprised them all when the announcer called my name as the winner of the competition. I can't lie, it surprised me too. I was more than overjoyed to have won such an honor and more importantly a small scholarship and the chance to compete again the following year in a statewide competition, which I lost. After my senior year in high school, I went on to Tuskegee. Not without running away from home first and constantly getting into it with my mother about everything. I was more than ready to leave the nest. I still didn't have all the money I needed for school and Timmy and I had broken up after his infidelity with a chick from his unit, which he told me about, over breakfast at a crowded restaurant.

I was still determined to get the hell out of my mom's house, and she had made it clear that she desired the same result. By the fall of 2001, I was on my way from Illinois to Alabama with my family driving me down to drop me off. They had not participated in the admission process so many mistakes were made on my part and when we arrived, I discovered that my tuition wasn't paid, and I would need to take out additional loans to secure housing and meals. When they left, I couldn't tell them that I was in such a horrible position financially. I was, in their eyes, an adult and no longer their concern.

I started to, once again, search for ways to not go back home and to financially take care of my own problems, my own education, and to support myself. Stuck in Tuskegee, but playing the college girl well for any spectators, I joined the cheer-leading team, the tennis team, and participated in the model troop and pageants. Going to class was last on my list. I was focused on trying to understand the culture, trying to fit in, to belong, and boys. For once I was getting lots of attention from Black boys and this meant more to me than anything. I was ages away from my party line days when all I could do was converse on my parent's kitchen phone.

With my scholarships and loans not fulfilling my financial obligations I began to look for easy ways of making cash. My short pageant stint and my model troop experience made me believe I had a real chance at pursuing modeling. Not as a career but to an end. It meant that I wouldn't have to go back home. I typed in Adult modeling agency. I was after all, an adult and I wanted to model. I found an agency and contacted them immediately. The agency owner advised me that I need photos, a head-shot and comp cards. I got right to work. With every photo sent, he would ask for more and more revealing photos. I would comply. After much back and forth, the agency agreed to take me on as a model. I was overly excited and made the call home to tell my mother that I was leaving school to be a model and that I would be going to New York to do so.

Her laughter was all I needed to fuel my determination. I had no clue what I was doing but anything was better than returning home to her. I packed my bags and took my first greyhound to the big apple. With my bags full of makeup, clothes I learned to wear from watching others, and with my new-found obsession, (weave and full wigs), I caught the first bus from Chicago to New York. It was the longest trip of my life. I never thought we would make it. This was the only way I could think of that would help me escape my overbearing mother and help me define my own beauty. With college behind me now, after a holiday break turned escape, as a failed attempt at adulting and changing the educational threshold for my entire family, I thought this was something easy to do where others were successful and where the road seemed simple. I was naive, sheltered, and unaware of the realities of the world. Stepping off the bus with my arms full of my untidy belongings, I reached for the first thing I could grab to keep me from falling. I reached out my hand, to steady myself.

Without realizing it, I had touched my hand on the gentleman standing directly beside me. I didn't notice him standing there until I gathered my balance only to feel his hurried brush of my hand away from his shoulders. "Don't put your hands on me bitch," he yelled. I stood there in total disbelief. Why was he being so mean? I hadn't had much experience with men during my high school years. My interactions with boys consisted of conversations on "the party line" and "Black Planet". I had only superficial relationships that never surpassed the surface when it came to actually opening up to anyone or knowing what to do in a quality friendship.

I attracted boys who came with no real concern for first loves or the thrills of childhood romances. Still nothing could have prepared me for this rude man. Now that I think about it, during the bus ride, someone was talking loudly. I think they were on their phone. Must've had free nights and weekends because they were in no hurry to end their vulgar discussion. Every other word was a curse word and I just got sick and tired of it. I shouted out, to the passenger, "can you please be quiet." I think this man I had grabbed onto, was now the passenger staring me in my face.

"Excuse me, sir," I replied to the stumpy man wearing a full bubble winter coat and Timberland boots. He gazed at my small frame, looking me up and down, sizing me up. Before he walked away, he spit on the ground, looked up at me, and said, "you in New York now bitch." I was so scared. I thought for sure he'd pull out a gun or slap the taste out of my mouth. I can't really be mad. Innocent little me, I was now in New York to start my modeling career. I needed money and I needed it fast. I wanted to move out and have my own life and follow my own dreams without being controlled.

It was this sense of urgency that led me to search for job openings that offered the most money for an 18-year-old girl. By this time, I was operating fully on autopilot. I made dumb decision after dumb decision. I still didn't know what I wanted to, really, do with my life, but I knew it was not working a regular 9 to 5. I can't tell you why, it was impossible for me to find any sort of comfort working to fulfill anyone's goals but my own. If I was going to do that, it would be quick fast and easy.

He appealed to my innocence, played on my insecurities, and made promises of good fortune. I should have had more integrity than this. I should have known better, but the goal was to be free to make my own decisions without judge nor jury, by any means necessary. It's even difficult for me to tell you this, years later, in letter form. I know that to free myself of the pain felt from my past, I must be honest even when I'd rather not. I didn't think anyone would ever see them. I was a nobody and porn is the last place anyone would expect to see me pop up. This was the dumbest excuse I'd given myself, but I slept just fine at night. I can honestly say I have no clue why I did adult videos; I'd desperately like to blame that on my anxiety or depression.

I remember walking through the mall once. I was always alone after the videos surfaced. A grown man stopped me to question me about the videos. This was not the type of attention I desired. Most of all, I let my mother down. Not away from my parent's protection longer than 6 months and I have already ruined my life. I experience emotional hurt like most relate physical pain. I crawled under my bed and held in my cry. Everyone knew, the people at church, people I went to high school with, the pageant I previously won was requesting their scholarships back. I became the most defensive version of myself from that moment. I never went outside without my shield of protection again. I blocked every blessing, fearful that they didn't come in peace. After I returned home, I was different. Damaged. I even looked different to myself.

My decisions branded me a failure. Every visit to the mirror ushered in my self-persecution. People were no longer people to me. They were pawns on a game-board. I would need to learn how to move and manipulate every piece so that I could control every interaction with everyone. I was never to be my true self again. I had made my decision. I was feeling all types of emotions. I knew what I needed to do but just not how to do it.

* * *

I lifted my head from my hands to take account of my location. It was as if I had slipped into a trance and now my recovery time was TBD. I heard her shuffling the phone as she began to speak again, "Chelle, come and get your son. Get your belongings out of my dryer and you need to get yourself together. Come now," she said with the urgency of a scorned lover. I pressed end on the call and tossed the phone into the passenger's seat.

I was still sitting on the shoulder on the expressway and I needed to move. Cars were speeding by and my concentration was so screwed up that I couldn't even merge back into traffic. I decided to ride the shoulder and exit at the next sign. *I could make a quick stop on my way home,* I thought to myself. I turned the dial on the radio to my favorite Chicago station. With Jill bellowing out her sweat melodies through my speakers, I was back in my comfort zone. Me and my music, and the wind. I loved it when it was warm outside. There was nothing like rolling your window down and jamming to some good music, and cruising in Illinois. I was off the expressway now. Jill was still killing her song. She was giving me every bit of my life, helping me drive this car up the street to my ex boyfriend's building. Well, he wasn't really my ex-boyfriend. I don't really know what to call him, but I partially blame him for me losing my mind right now. Have you ever had a man mess with your brain so much that you end up questioning and doubting your own intelligence? Well that was him.

I told him, Deidrick, I'd come over and pick up the rest of my boxes by 2pm and from a glance at my phone, I could see that, it was almost 1:30. I had one missed call and one new text message. It was Deidrick. He was one of the very few men that I could say I was attracted to. The last time I saw him didn't leave me with a good taste in my mouth. The last time we saw each other, he was arriving to the apartment I rented from him, accompanied by his new girlfriend, while he and I were still sleeping together from time to time. He probably met this chick online and now he was driving from Cali to Chicago with old girl. I pretended like I didn't care when he told me about her. He insisted that he previously informed me that we were just friends, but I don't fuck my friends, I got a kid, and I'm too old to be playing these damn kiddie games. I guess I was thinking since we were still sleeping together then we must be working towards building something bigger. That's what I get for thinking I had all the answers. I'll just be glad to get my son's toys and the rest of my clothes.

The message on my phone read, "bring the key". I grabbed the key from my back pocket as I pulled into his driveway. I made sure not to roll on the grass as he has warned me not to do on numerous occasions. He owned a Queen Anne style home, nestled in a quiet neighborhood. When I lived there, I would take Roan on walks to the park. Deidrick and I went on a few late-night walks ourselves. As much as I loathed him, part of me still loved him. That was my problem. I loved everyone no matter the wrong they did to me. This alone will be the death of me. He was young, 28, but he was all about acquiring wealth, being able to travel the world freely, and hoes, he was about having sex with as many women as possible and as often as possible. You couldn't blame him though. He was only doing what us women, allowed.

We met online, on a dating app. It was one of the apps where you like them and connect if they like you as well. We connected, began chatting and set up a date for later that week. He said, "it's a waste of time going back and forth with each other, let's just meet in person." I was eager to meet up because I was lonely. I played coy and tried to prolong our online chatting, but he was serious about meeting up. I wasn't initially attracted to him. When he picked me up for our first date on that cold and snowing February afternoon,

I went above and beyond to look my best for him and for me too. I wanted to feel pretty. I got my hair done for the first time in over a year. I stopped at the mall on my way home from the beauty shop. I bought a plush, turtleneck sweater. I did my makeup carefully because the sweater was white, and I didn't want to get anything on it.

He was on the cute spectrum somewhere. Where, I wasn't sure. He was the type that you could fix. His hairline was already receding, but this was fixable. His car was a small bug style car. The appearance of company logos on his windshield gave away his side hustle. I could tell from the inside of his car that he was a five-star driver that served mints and water to his riders. I like nerds and he was the epitome of just that, I thought. He didn't plan the date well. Took me to the local casino. I played with my own money. We had drinks and grabbed a bite to eat after we returned from showing his potential tenants his rental property. I paid for the food because he said he wasn't hungry. I hadn't eaten all day preparing for the date with him. I tried to make the best of my botched date. There was chemistry so we went back to his place. I don't know what I expected from him. I was obviously eager and wanted the attention.

His foreplay was amazing. He made me feel like he really was into me. The next day I returned to his house for breakfast per his request. He wanted me to come over without make-up on. I was hesitant but lonely, so I went. He made me feel comfortable with no foundation on my face and with my disheveled hair from yesterday's game of "hide and go get it." That was all it took for me to be hooked. Attention. Lies. And sex. This lasted for a short period before he began canceling dates, making excuses for not communicating and for the many women he lied to me about. We ended our, whatever it was. We started talking again, even after all of his bullshit, because my car was towed, I needed a ride from work, he picked me up, and one car ride later, we were at his place and he was doing things to my body again that stirred an awakening in my soul. His energy, when we were making love was intoxicating. All of this had led us to this day more than a year later.

"Hey, you," he said, removing the phone from his face for only a moment. He brushed my arm with his hand. I looked down to the ground and hid my face. "Hey", I replied softly as I tried to hold back my smile. I was genuinely happy to see him. I tried not to stare too long at his muscular physique, but he was walking along side of me now as I made my way to the bedroom. "Give me a second," he whispered.

I wanted to tell him no but what came out was, "OK." I started to look for anything that belonged to me or Roan. The house was a fixer upper. Deidrick purchased the property a few years ago and was slowly renovating the two apartments. The upstairs, where we lived, looked like two rooms, a piece of a bathroom, and a makeshift kitchen all slapped together with a closet for a living room. "You have stuff everywhere, literally everywhere," I said jokingly. This was my attempt to engage him in conversation since he was no longer on the phone. "

Why don't you help me clean it up," he said flirtatiously. "This feels like a setup," I replied. "Oh, you will know when I'm setting you up," he went on. I was standing at the edge of his bed now. He was sitting on the side of it, in front of me. Still totally naked. This used to be my bed but now he's sleeping in it with other women. "Come here, he says gently, pulling me near his naked frame. I closed my eyes as I felt my body begin to melt and merge into his familiar embrace, "I can't do this to myself," I whispered, as I carefully pushed him away.

This was all happening in slow motion. My heart and my mind were now in two different energy zones and I was about to lose control. Grabbing my wrist with his hand, he pulled me back toward him. I could feel the heat in between our bodies rising. "You look so good right now," he mumbled. Half-way believing what he said, I brought my eyes into focus and contacted his. I had developed the habit of not looking people in their eyes, when I spoke to them, over the years. This could have been a direct result of the abusive relationships, low self-esteem, or my genuine shyness that contributed to my new habit, I really didn't know why. I knew he would see that I was serious in this moment because I wouldn't allow him to escape the entrancing gaze of my eyes.

"Deidrick, boy let me go. I have a lot of stuff to do today and I'm already frustrated." I tried to pull away to make him think I didn't really want to be bothered but the truth in the matter is that I did want to be bothered. I needed this attention, this affection.

"The last time I saw you, was when you were bringing Kayla here and I'm still dealing with that," I said softly.

"Come on, you got to get over that," he shot back at me. "I'm young and enjoying life, you know what this is," he said.

"I'm done fighting you," I told him, reminding him of the missed calls, texts left with no reply, the late nights standing in the window wondering when he was going to pop up, if he was going to pop up, the time we were making love and his ex-wife walked in and watched us before I could get the chance to even cover myself. I reminded him of the times he needed me, and I was there, of the times when all he wanted was sex and I knew it, but I gave in anyway. I reminded him of all this knowing I was to blame for allowing myself to stay in this situation.

I slowly pulled away from his grasp. Touched his shoulders with my hands and whispered into his ear, "not today buddy." I had reached my limit. I didn't want to play any more cat and mouse games with him. Besides, I had other things to think about. I packed a few things and left. I left most of the important pieces behind. I forget to grab Roan's piano, some of his action figures and my hair-care products for a business I was trying to start. I was pissed that I allowed myself to get distracted, but things happen, so I told myself I'd get it later as I drove away towards my parents' house.

* * *

I moved back home to live with my parents. It was the hardest decision I'd had to make in a very long time. I know that you're supposed to be able to rely and depend on family, but we just don't operate that way. I hadn't looked at my phone for a while now. Something was telling me not to look at it. I drove in silence, windows down, not caring if the wind played beautician with my short strands that resembled curls from far distances. I was just driving and thinking. Upset with myself for allowing Deidrick to penetrate my thoughts when I knew he didn't deserve to be there.

The 20-minute drive from his house to my parents was depressing to say the lease. I dreaded pulling into the cul de sac. I could feel my body beginning to freeze up from the fear of the shit storm I was walking into. My palms begin to drip again. I parked in the driveway, as I normally did, on the left side, in front of the garage so someone could park behind me, enter and exit the garage with ease, and just in case someone needed to park beside me. These were the house rules and just like wash days are assigned, so are parking spots. There was no feeling of community in our home only dictatorship, chaos and turmoil. We had developed this way of living among one another, over time.

I dreaded this part of my life and I'm almost sure my facial expressions told the truths my lips wouldn't tell. My legs felt weaker than usual. Approaching the open garage, I shuffled past my mother's truck and into the house. I hated coming here. They had worked their whole life to build this home and although I was proud of them, it didn't take away from them making my life a living hell while my son and I sought refuge. This is where we ran to live, when Deidrick showed up with his new girlfriend. I can't say that it took me by surprise. I had a few weeks to prepare, once he told me that he was bringing someone back and he wanted his place back. I was just stuck after that. It was like I got up every day just to go back to bed. I didn't plan or anything.

I allowed depression to take over as I slowly faded to the background in my own life. I lost my job a few months before and I couldn't bring myself to tell him. When I couldn't pay the rent, he told me I had to leave. I hated that job anyway. I only took it to shut my parents up. I was working at the post office, where humans go to die. I told my mom that I was laid off. She just kept asking me every day, "what you gone do Chelle?" I told her I would figure something out. I made no attempt to figure anything out. I knew that I could always go home, and I was holding on to hope that Deidrick would return with some type of sympathy for me and my son. Now I had to leave all of that behind. I was giving myself a few more days to clean out my belongings from his apartment then I was going to be done with him for good.

* * *

Cry Where You Are.

I cry into the mirror, so I can see myself.
So that I may, acknowledge my own pain and release my own suffering.
The ache that accompanies the cry is the most uncomfortable.
inking into this bathroom floor, becoming one with the steam streaked mirror.
Paint chips, Hand Towels, Coconut oil.
I can't leave.
Waiting for my reflection to reflect that in which I long to see.
I'm ashamed of me.
I have to stop doing this.
This is where I own up to my failures and move on.
This is where I let go of my insecurities.
This is where
I cry into the mirror, so I can see myself.

I cried in the bed this morning.
I woke up after sleeping all moon.
I was sleepwalking again.
Awake and afraid to be alive.
I didn't get up.
Just laid there, and cried.
The ache that accompanies the cry is the most uncomfortable.
Neglect becomes child to my sorrow.
I forgot to eat again.
Melting into the Kitchen floor.

Cold water, eat a cracker, coconut oil.
Dragging dead bodies across thresholds into my bedroom.
I can't leave.
I'm ashamed of me.
I have to stop doing this. I've outgrown this indolence.
I'm aware of my strength.
Yet and still I cried in the bed this morning,

I cry every time he hurts me.
Convoluted truths meet me at the door knob.
Forcing my fears and insecurities to the surface.
Realizing my sacrifices were, sacrifices.
The ache that accompanies the cry is the most uncomfortable.
Melting into the door frame.
Infidelities, cars, condoms.
Unspoken promises, broken.
I can't leave.
Say something, say nothing.
Ask me to stay, say nothing.
I'll stay.
I'm ashamed of me.
I have to stop doing this. Infancy revealed his offering.
Instability his offspring.
The inevitable is inevitable yet,
I cry every time he hurts me.

I eventually stop crying.
Cleaning the window for new rain and steam stains.
Temporary distractions to dull all pain.
The ache that accompanied the cry was the most uncomfortable.
Flowing in the spirit of everywhere.
Wet, silent, peaceful now.
Repetition completed.

By peace was defeated.
I can't leave.
Coming to terms with my reality.
Appreciating the sobriety.
Forgiveness succeeds, after all,
I eventually stop crying.

A Father's Daughter

I was surprised to see police sitting inside of my parent's home when I arrived. I must've missed the cars parked outside. As I opened the door and stepped in, I saw what this was. Hurriedly, I began grabbing everything that belonged to Roan. I rushed upstairs and grabbed the clothing that was left in the laundry room. As I made my way back to the bottom of the stairs, one of the officers approached me.

"Rochelle can you just sit down and talk to us for a minute? We'd like to help you." He said.

Roan was playing in the living room and would occasionally make small-talk with the other officers so I had to play it cool. I placed the small bag and picture frame from the Detroit Zoo that held a torn picture of me and Ro' and the person who I used to be married to, down next to the door to indicate that my overall goal was to exit the premises and as soon as possible.

Sitting at the table was not only my parents but also my little sister. Six years between us, we'd never gotten along so I didn't understand why she was even there. I slid into the chair at the head of the table so I could see everyone and so I could quickly exit if needed. "What is this all about?" I asked the officer.

"Hi Rochelle, may I call you Rochelle? My name is Officer Schwartz. Your family is concerned about your behavior and they are genuinely worried about you and your son's well-being." He said.

"If they were really worried about us,then we wouldn't be in this situation and you wouldn't be here," I said. "Support goes a long way." I finished. My toes clenched tightly inside my boots, I folded my hands and placed them on the table. I leaned to one side of the chair and turned my attention directly towards Officer Schwartz.

"Did you write this note Rochelle?" He asked pulling a folded piece of paper from his closed fist.

The waters began to rise in my eyes. I held my breath and clinched my teeth before I replied. "Yes, I wrote the note," I told him.

"Why did you write this note, with these particular words Rochelle?" He asked, *matter-of-factly*.

Squeezing each individual finger until the knuckle echoed a loud popping sound I answered him. "That note was for my son." I told him.

"So how did your parents get the note?" He asked. "Because I gave it to Ro' a few days ago when my father and I had an argument. I left Ro' here with them (pointing toward my parents)."

"So you just left your son with your parents, with a note that reads, I'm sorry I wasn't strong enough. I love you. Please forgive me?" He asked.

"See, I told you she was slow." I heard my sister say.

I immediately rose from the table. Looking around the room, I could see that there was no advocate for me among these people and all I could think about was, *getting the hell out of there.* Standing with me now, was the officer. A few inches taller than me, his demeanor wasn't threatening and there was a calmness in his face. "Let's step outside and talk for a minute if you don't mind," he said, adding, "It's totally up to you. Since you wrote the note a few days ago and your son is healthy, you can absolutely leave and take your son with you. No one will stop you, but I think there is a deeper issue and I would like to offer you a listening ear and help, if I can."

I took him up on his offer and we both stepped outside onto the front porch. "Are you OK Rochelle?" He asked once we were outside, and the door had closed behind us.

"No I'm not, not in the least bit." I told him. "People go through shit. Life is hard and this is just me going through something right now." I replied.

"What are you going through?" He asked.

"I'm just tired. Tired of running into the same brick wall over and over again." I said. "I've been through a lot and I think I've reached a breaking point."

"Well you know your family is worried about you, they think you're a danger to yourself and to your son." He informed me.

"Maybe I am." I shot back. "If they would offer non judgmental help and would get off my back and support me more maybe I could handle all of this without breaking down." I advised him. I , different from the one who made such bad decisions, felt hostage to the consequences of her actions. Betrayed by my own adaptation of personalities I formed to please others, I led a sad and lonely life internally. It became easy, yet remained difficult, to be who others wanted me to be, who they thought I should be.

"What's your relationship like with your father?" He asked. "He seems really emotional over this." He finished.

"Believe it or not," I told him, "my father and I have been best friends since I was a little girl. We've always had a special bond. He's been the only one I can talk to for a while now. I don't really know how we got here." I said.

With endearing kindness, Officer Schwartz placed his arm on my shoulder. He said, "Maybe you do know Rochelle. Try and think about that for a moment.

Returning home, to my father's house after my New York, modeling fiasco, was not an easy task. Being there, in New York City was a trial that even law school couldn't have equipped me for. After that first porn exploitation situation, I decided to chill for a minute with going out on a limb and trying new ways to eat. I was just going to try to take my life back and find a more, legal and morally accepted way to stack some coins before I embarked on another unforgiving journey in search of independence and attempting to control the outcome of my own adulthood. I was, in many ways, still a child. Not quite twenty-one, but no longer eighteen.

The pictures were all over the place and had made its way back to my hometown. I felt recognized everywhere I went. even in the local mall.

I was being pushed into the underground world again, of sleazeballs and hustlers. They were already prepared to take advantage of a Black girl's innocence. The emails were flowing in one after the other. All boasting how their independent film was the next big thing and how they only needed me for one scene.

I chalked it up to easy money. I wasn't in any real relationship. My mother had always said, "When you get a boyfriend, I get a boyfriend." Needless to say, I never had a real one. No man lasted longer than three months with me. I was free to do as I pleased. I would meet up with guys sometimes and we'd go to dinner or a hotel and they'd pay me for my time. It never dawned on me that I was becoming a high-priced, call-girl.

I would pull up with my makeup kit and hooker uniform. It was fast and easy cash, although, there was always this little voice in the back of mind, saying, *"I really wish he'd hurry up."*

The men would send luxury cars to pick me up, have me booked in the best hotels, and would accommodate my needs and requests for what I was giving in return. I saw it as an even exchange. Although it was far from it. A few adds answered for call girls and XXX actresses and I was making more money in one month than I had ever made working at the movie theater or nursing home back during high school.

I was basically my own pimp. After hustling up enough money to go half on an apartment with my favorite white boy brother, J. I didn't really tell him where the money came from but there was word going around the neighborhood already. Even after I got a few jobs at a hotel and purchased some wheels, I couldn't reveal that the source of my income wasn't real professional modeling. I couldn't possibly tell him that here I was, a hoe before I was twenty-one.

A few videos in Vegas, later, I decided I couldn't live like this anymore. I had so many people in my life who had sought to forgive me time and time again. It was time to desire more for myself because I was free falling with immediate danger imminent. I still needed enough money so I could break into some type of career, become someone, or at least be able to afford college so I could qualify for some type of job. I needed money and nobody was going to help me. It was clear to me then, I'd have to help myself.

The last video I shot was with some guy I had just met named Will. We shot at someone's house, in their pool and on their pool table. He gave off good vibes and our chemistry, during the scenes was great. I made myself comfortable with him so he was all too willing to keep in contact after the job was done. That month, when the rent was due, I couldn't face J. because I knew that I was broke. I didn't have the money. I dropped everything and decided to make my luck in New York, one last time.

I packed my convertible. Oiled her up real good, and picked up a road map to accompany the mapquest directions I printed at the library. I told my parents that I was leaving town to give it another try. They were filled with questions and pleaded for me not to go. They withheld any financial support but waited until I told them I was driving my car to the courier for my mom to hand me forty dollars for gas. I told them that I would be flying to New York and they believed me. I told them some crazy lie, like, "I was going to have my car shipped to New York." I don't know why they actually bought that story, but they did. So I contacted Will. He said, "Everything was all set for my arrival." I made my way, enduring hills, mountains, and deer crossing the dark road in the dead of the night. I was cruising all of the back roads alone with my top down and it was scary to say the least. I had to get there.

With my map in hand, it was nearly noon when I arrived, after driving all night and stopping for gas and snacks only, I was excited to be there. I had only made it to an airport exiting ramp, when the car began to overheat. I hadn't made it to my final destination. Nonetheless, I found myself, stalled, dead smack in the middle of the off-ramp. Still, there was no stopping me. I found a phone, called Will and had him and one of his boys meet me with some bottles of oil and coolant and we popped the hood and went to work.

I was excited once we made it to his quietly tucked away building. In, what I assumed was Brooklyn or Queens. A quick glance into his place and I could already tell that he lived with someone. A female someone. I wasn't going to be in some strangers home. Without hesitation, I asked him.

"Do you live with someone? I mean, what's the plan?" I asked him. I was bringing in the bags of clothes and setting them over in the corner. Where Will had motioned for me to place them. It was back in the bedroom. There I followed his directions.

He was tall and full of exposed mussels. His body, his demeanor, his structure was intimidating. "Don't worry about this house," he said. "All you need to worry about is this work I've booked for you." He finished.

His face told a story different from the one conveyed by his voice over the phone.

"As a matter of fact," he yelled into the room, "eat, take a nap, do what you got-to-do, because tonight, I have a job for you." He said.

I knew something was weird about him from the way his voice was so hard when he spoke to me. It was like he was barking orders to a dog the way he huffed out each syllable. I was uneasy but I was here so I'd have to see this through. There was no way I could call home after 24 hours and say I'd failed again. I had to see this through.

Stepping out in my best gear from a West side girl who got her style from watching music videos and XOXO ads in fashion magazines, I quickly found out that I wasn't prepared for New York nightlife. Not one bit.

"I had you an oil change done." He said, as we approached my car. He didn't have a car and I didn't dare ask him if he had a driver's license so we were rolling. When we pulled into the parking lot there were a few drunks arguing and, from my count, a few prostitutes. I could see them standing up against the wall. I had no clue where he had taken us. we walked into what looked like a waiting area. I could hear what sounded like roller rink music going on inside. I figured it was an industry party. He pushed me to the side, looking me directly in my eye he said stand over here and be quiet.

I've never been quiet in my life but something told me to shut the hell up and start figuring a way out of this before we die. Just then,the manager, or man who I learned to be one of the owners later, approached Will and they spoke for a moment. Then Will walked back over to me and began his introduction.

"This is Shelly." He said, putting my hand into the owners as we greeted each other then Will handed him some cash. As soon as the transaction was done and I was now in the hands of the owner, he ushered me back behind the curtains that separated the waiting area from the room where I heard the music earlier.

I heard Will shout, "I'll be back at 4 to pick you up." Then he was gone.

Pink, red, black revealing stripper outfits, were being thrown in my face. "What size do you wear?" One girl asked me. She was the one the owner had put in charge of showing me the ropes.

*What the f*** have I gotten myself into? I* thought to myself.

"Just pick one." She instructed me. "Now that's your locker. Here is the main stage and here are the private rooms." She went on as I tried to take it all in. It was hitting me all at once. Smack-dead in my face. *I guess I'm a stripper now.* I thought to myself; *So this is what it's come to?*

I learned the ropes quickly that night. I learned which bouncer was cool and how much I needed to tip the DJ to play black music that I could dance to. I probably walked out with two hundred bucks. it wasn't a lot but it was more than I walked in there with and all I had to do was gyrate on a man's crotch to get it.

Will picked me up. He didn't speak the entire way back to his place and a glance at the gas tank said he'd been bending corners in my whip but I didn't dare cause trouble. When we arrived I got comfortable removing my nasty girl garments and cleansing my skin. I didn't want him to get crazy but I had to ask, "why would you make a commitment for me to dance somewhere, not ask me if it's something I want to do, and leave me somewhere without my car alone?" I yelled toward the front room.

As I turned the corner, he met me at the living room entrance. "You're in my house." He said. "You do what I say and how I say it." he raised his voice so the neighbors could hear him now. While forcing his fists to make contact with the wall nearest my head.

I was taken back. I knew that the situation could only get worse if I reacted in the wrong way. I backed out of the room slowly.

"Okay Will," I said, "I hear you." I said. "Okay Will." I repeated.

Realizing my retreat, he continued to pounce. "Where is the money you made tonight? How much did you make?" He asked. He reached out his hand, motioning for me to give it here.

I walked over to my bag sitting on top of the trash bag full of clothes on the floor, in the corner. I pulled out a stack of bills and handed them to him.

"You must take me for a clown Nigga." He said, tossing the bills into my face.

"What the fuck is this bullshit?" He barked.

The bills seemed frozen in mid-air as his arm stretched across my face, I stood there, also frozen, as they glided slowly to the ground. It was as if time was standing still. I watched him walk quickly to the head of the bed and reached under his pillow. I had never seen a gun up close before.

"I hope you don't take me for no dummy Nigga." He was raising his voice again. "The next time I send you somewhere, you better come back with all my money." He said, while holding the gun near my chest.

"I'm not okay." I said. "I hear you. You don't have to scream at me." Fearful but pissed off more than anything, I continued twisting my body and rolling my neck. "What makes you think it's okay to put me in a situation like that in the first place? Before I got up here we said we'd be partners. I'm not dumb either." I told him. "You just don't treat people like that. I don't know what you think this is. Now, I'm going to bed. Don't talk to me and don't touch me. What time do you need me to go to the club tomorrow?" I asked him.

"Nine." He mumbled as I walked off and prepared for bed. I locked myself in the bathroom and slid down the back of the door. Landing in a puddle of my own silent screams. That night, I didn't sleep. I felt him creeping into the bed beside me. I made a line in the blankets with my hand and pulled the covers tight around my body leaving no room for him to enter my space.

The following days, I played the role and put all my attention into learning the ropes. I was doing more talking than dancing at the club but somehow I managed to pull two or three Champagne Room dances a night. Mostly, I was meeting people and trying to find someone I could trust.

He came 3 days later but it wasn't a moment too soon. He wanted to talk, wanted to know where I was from and what I was doing dancing at a juice bar in New York City. I told him everything. Something about his innocent face told me, I could trust him. The music was loud but he was leaning in close, hanging on my every word.

The past two nights, Will told me to get a ride from one of the girls so I didn't hesitate to accept once he offered me a ride back to where I was staying. I changed from my seductive stripper wear and resurfaced now stuffing my bones into some skin tight flare jeans, a baby doll top, and a Baby Phat jacket with the matching heels.

I walked out front to meet him. He was leaning against what looked like, an undercover cop car. "Get in." He said. "Don't act all shy now. I'm not going to kidnap you. You couldn't stop talking a minute ago. Come on, let me take you home." He opened the door and motioned for me to take my time. I sat in the passenger seat and as he walked around to the driver's door, I reached over and swung it open for him.

"I knew you were a good one." He said. We both laughed. "So where are we going? He asked.

"I can't say that I know the address." I told him. "But, I can get us there." We both laughed again. We drove. His eyes were on the road while I scanned the car, my eyes jumping from the computer and display screens to the gun clearly visible now, on his waist. "Tell me more about this Will. How many clips does he have?" Tommy began asking more detailed questions. It hit me that he wasn't planning on dropping me off and I was grateful.

He stood behind me as I knocked on Will's door. This knock was different. It wasn't my normal tap. I was knocking with authority. Will looked through the peephole and swung the door open. I stepped into the apartment, moving quickly towards the bedroom that stored my belongings. As Will pushed the door closed behind me, we both stopped and turned towards the door as the base and force booming from Tommy's voice interrupted the commotion.

"Aye Yo Son," he said, sticking his foot through the door opening and forcing the door back on Will. "Yo son, she's about to get her things and bounce. We can have beef if you want it to go down like that or you can chill." He said with the lift of his black tea exposing his gun and badge. "Do we have any problems? Get your shit and let's go Rochelle."

Tommy was looking at me but standing with his hands clasped together as he stood in front of Will, blocking his view from me. "And give me her car keys and anything else you got of hers and stay the fuck away from her." He told him as we both grabbed my bags and made our way to the car. With Will still standing there, we drove my car to Tommy's and parked it.

"You want to go to a diner?" All of that just went on and I couldn't believe that he was thinking about food. We were back in Tommy's car. Just as he finished his questions I felt myself thinking, *he's cute, maybe* it's just the light from the display screen making the diamond studs protruding from his ears, twinkle. His handsomeness more evident, with his high cheekbones and honey complexion causing my focus to shift from the danger we barely had avoided, I caught myself before I allowed myself to slip.

"Sure I could eat." I told him. I wasn't in a hurry to be alone and for the first time in days, I felt safe. We joked over a plate of fried calamari, about how I've never eaten it before and how gooey they were. "Thank you for tonight" I told him. He reached out and grabbed my hand.

"You deserve to have someone that always got your back, especially out here." He went on. "You trying to do whatever this is by yourself. I couldn't leave you out here hanging."

We stopped off to check on his elderly grandfather before we made it back to my car. He told me he knew a cheap hotel in Queens where I could check in right now. I followed him there. He helped me bring in my bags, checked out the room and made sure that I knew how to lock the door. I thanked him. we exchanged information, then I was alone again.

Left to my own devices and in New York for a purpose unlike that of my first time here, I knew I had to get it together. I settled into the hole in the wall room in the rundown mom-and-pop piece of a hotel. I decided to sleep for the day and gather myself for the road ahead. I knew I couldn't go back to the club. That meant I'd have to figure out a way to make money for gas, food, and to stay in this raggedy Motel.

I used my calling cards to contact some of the girls from the club. I didn't tell anyone where I was staying but they were well informed on all of the clubs hiring new girls, which led me to a place in Queens. I worked my way around the club scene. I got so good at playing the role, I thought, that I found myself working three clubs at once. Every dime went to what I was going to eat, where I was going to stay, gas in my car, and finding real modeling work. Nights at the club where eventful, to say the least. I met every category of men that you could think of. Some of them wanted to take me home. Some of them wanted to enjoy the fantasy and I was equipped to provide. I adapted and learned the ropes more and more now.

It wasn't long before I was tipping the DJ extra the play my favorite songs that will help me escape the reality that I was taking off the small amount of clothes I had on, in the middle of a stage, surrounded by a room full of men, whose only goal was to be sexually stimulated. I spent my evenings drinking whiskey sours and picking one or two men to provide a fantasy along with a big tip at the end of the night.

I got friendly with the house moms at each of the clubs and they all looked out for me. A few weeks after dancing for my dinner, a few of the girls called me over to their section in the VIP room. Surrounded by red lights and floating drones of light, flashing, all around the room, the music was blasting and we could barely hear one another. There was a girl in the cage dancing for dollars and taking shots. I settled into my seat, as the extrovert leaned in and whispered in my ear. "This guy is cool. He wants us to go to a model call with him tomorrow." I was living from hotel to customers beds and I was hungry. I agreed to meet up with them at his place. I lied to my parents long enough. It was time to take chances and risks.

Making our way past a velvet rope and a few suited gatekeepers, we descended beneath a modern office building and entered what seemed to be, a very British gentlemen's club. The decor was library through and through. Polished wooden floors, Oriental rugs, velvet and silk overstuffed couches, damask-fringed draperies, marble fireplaces with brass accouterments. Even antique wooden shelves filled with the classics. Only an upward glance at the black-ducted ceiling will bring you back to reality. The crowd was a mix of very barely dressed young ladies, and men on the older side, dressed in suits.

We were seated at different tables. The people that I had showed up with were seated at one table and I at another. Our meals were brought out in course order. We only had a selection between chicken or pork. There were men all around me and beautiful women who look like they had waited their entire life for moments just as this one. Then it hit me. I was in the moment that I have been waiting for. Surrounded by agents models and industry people alike, I was where I wanted to be.

The music was playing and no one was dancing but I couldn't stop tapping my feet. The man sitting next to me, with his feminine voice, called over to me. At least, I thought he was talking to me.

"Hey girl, brown skin, you want to dance?" He asked.

"Sure." I responded. "I don't see why not." I said, as we hit the floor. Taking my hand in his, he swung me around and we began to dance to the up-tempo music, playing in the background. It was as if everyone else in the room had disappeared. He was feeling his thing and I was feeling mine. I was excited. I felt comfortable for the first time in New York City. After dancing and dancing we returned to our table and began to talk about who we were and where we were from. There was something familiar about him and he said the same about me. He said, "it was easy for him to talk to me and that he could see me in films and entertainment and doing interviews."

We laughed. It was great. By the end of the night I was laughing and joking with agents and managers. They were all in search of the next big thing. I was dancing and eating. I wasn't a ditsy model and it showed. Scott that was his name, from Sub-Zero Model Management, looked at me and said, "Get away from that crowd you're in and if you really want it, if you really want to work, maybe tomorrow I will find you on white and Canal where I operate Sub-Zero Model Management."

"Okay." I told him. "I'll be there." I didn't know how to find him or if he'd be a pimp like the many other men I had encountered while in New York but I had to give it a shot. I literally had nothing to lose. With all the money I had left over now in my gas tank, I made my way to White and Canal to search for Scott, the following day. Upon my arrival, It was clear from the loft style office, that his operation was much smaller than he let on. The pretty black girl with high cheekbones at the desk, told me to have a seat, as she pointed to a row of black fold out chairs lined adjacent to the wall.

After waiting for some time and finally entering his office we sat down to have a chat. He gave me a look over and told me some things that he would fix. Told me we'd have to get a professional to do my hair. He said I needed to go shopping for makeup. He said I should lay off the bread and bagels. We laughed about how wild and crazy it was for me to pick up and leave my family back at home. He felt like a friend that I could confide in. He said that I could come to the studio as often as possible and try to pick up and learn as I pursued my passion. As feminine and flamboyant as he was. I had never met anyone that made me feel so welcomed and so free to be myself and not to feel bad for the decisions I had made before. We began to hang out and he began to send me on cold Cattle Calls.

He helped me create a portfolio and upgraded my look from a 4.5 to a 7.9. He showed me how to walk like I was making love. He showed me how to hold my head up and walk with my shoulders back. He gave me pointers on heels and we went shopping for makeup together, learning my complexion together. He couldn't promise me work. He said that I was not your average girl but I was not your New York girl either. I didn't take his words lightly and I didn't take them to heart. I knew that any criticism that came from him was guidance and not judgment. Over the time of him sending me to different casting calls, auditions, and extra rolls, I continued to dance at several clubs in the city.

I received my first extra role in a Spike Lee film that was shooting in the meatpacking district. It was a great experience. I had a lot of fun and I was able to send my checks home to my dad and he even framed it next to a picture of me. For once I was doing something that I loved but I wasn't making that much money so of course I was still dancing. Caught up in the world of trying to meet new people, learn the craft and industry, and trying to stay alive, I spent more time in the club than I would have liked to. Doing more things than I wanted to. But things that I thought would be needed for my survival.

There was one night when I was working in the club in Queens. One of the patrons was receiving a lot of attention from staff and even the girls. I paid him little to no attention though because I had no clue who he was. As I walked past him, he grabbed my hand and asked me to sit next to him. I accommodated his request because I was a dancer nonetheless. We spoke for a while and he asked me if I was hungry. He was a mobster. An old Italian. The kind of guy who was only good for two pumps and a roll. I didn't think much of him so of course I agreed for dinner after dancing.

His name was Augustine. He met me out front while sitting in his black Mercedes Benz. We asked one of the girls to drive my car home to make it easier for me to drive with him. He was a wrinkly old man. About 60 years old. One glance at him and I could tell what he was all about. He was one of those older men who like younger women and like to do things with them that were disgusting in my eyes. We went out to dinner and I had a couple of laughs. He told me all about how he had just gotten released from prison and how he was a part of organized crime.

I told him about my modeling dreams and how I was just a Suburban girl from Illinois. I told him how I was staying from couches to sofas of people I was just meeting and how I knew no one in the city really. He felt sorry for me and started making plans out loud.

"You can move in with me." He said. "I have a place in North-port Long Island. I'm building an addition right now. You should come check it out."

I didn't take him seriously but I was intrigued to know more. "I don't mind the drive." I said.

"Okay let's go." He said. We packed up our meals and made our way to his Mercedes Benz. He opened up my car door and was a very sweet gentleman. He made it very clear that he wanted more from me. More than just a one-night stand. I was alone and I needed help and I knew it. So I didn't mind his company. Not at all. I could see that he had money from the way he was waving the stacks of bills as he paid for dinner. It will be a lie if I didn't say that my motive was not to acquire some of his wealth.

I moved into his place in North-port Long Island. We went on vacations within a short period of time. I met his friends and he was financing my dreams. I wasn't dancing as much but I had become more of his house servant. I was there to please every need and every desire that he had. After a few weeks of this, I was over it. I was done. the payment was no longer worth the reward. One day, when he was out, I placed all of my clothing and all of my belongings into my convertible. I took his water jug full of coins and rolled it into my car. I didn't have any money of my own so I took what I could find in a hurry. I drove all the way back to Queens, not knowing where I was going and stopped at the club just to catch my breath.

My fluorescent blue Chrysler LeBaron was easy to spot in an indoor garage. Augustine must have been looking for me because he arrived at the club, took the coins out of the car and threatened me, inside the club. I barely escaped jumping into my convertible and speeding out of the lot looking over my shoulder to make sure I wasn't being followed. I drove all night not knowing where I was going and finally decided to call my mother to let her know I needed to come home.

I called my mom from a pay phone and told her what was going on and she asked where all my money was from the movies that I was doing. I told her that I needed to pay my expenses and I lost my lodging. She said she'd wire me $50 and she wouldn't have anymore for a while so I shouldn't ask. I thanked her and told her that would be enough. I found a wire transfer location and a small convenience shop and I parked my car outside until they would open the next morning.

Distraught, lost, and confused, my heart began to race as I sat in the car waiting. I began to question why I was alive. I began to doubt that I knew what I was doing. And I didn't think that anybody cared. I felt like I was going to pass out right there in the car and I didn't think anyone would find my body if I just dyed here.

Across the street, was a hospital. I could see people going in and out of the building and ambulances arriving. The thought crossed my mind that they would find my body. But again I began to doubt that they would find me in time. I crossed the street and made my way to the sidewalk towards the hospital. I walked through the doors and as the light hit my face I felt my body melt into the floor as I dropped and lost consciousness.

I was carried into the hospital and placed on a stretcher. They began to remove my clothes and ran a line for an IV. They begin to run test as I lied there weak and lifeless. After hours of receiving IV fluids and the hospital running test that rendered no answers, I spoke to an orderly or and x-ray technician, who told me they would be releasing me soon. I had no clue what time it was and I didn't feel better but I knew that I couldn't stay there. I didn't have insurance.

The technician stayed in my room, next to my bed. He was a six foot five, dark brown skin man and he told me his name was Ray John. He enjoyed his work and enjoyed meeting people and told me that he was genuinely concerned about my well-being. He asked me if I was okay? I told him I was and I nodded my head. He told me he wasn't taking that for an answer. That it wasn't good enough. That I needed to dig deeper. He said, "Something's going on with you and I know it. I think I'm going to sit here until either they discharge you or you tell me the truth." He said, I laughed.

I looked him in his eyes and I said. "Trust me you don't want to know."

It came time for the hospital to discharge me. It, subsequently, was also time for Ray John to end his shift. He followed me to my car and saw that I had bags exploding out of the windows filled with my belongings. He shook his head and said, "We're going to leave this here. I want you to get in my car, trust me you can trust me Rochelle, then I'm going to take care of you."

I could have burst into tears right then and there. It was just too good to be true. But after picking up the $50 my mom had sent via wire transfer, I didn't have any other plans and I was along for the ride anyway so I jumped in the truck with him and he took me home.

We sat down and talked and got to know each other. He told me that he was attracted to me but he was in a relationship, but something in him wanted to protect me and I desperately needed to be protected. He made me contact my parents. He made sure that I could connect with family members that my mother had in Jamaica Queens. After I connected with them and slept on their couch for a few weeks, Ray John, continued to visit me and to make sure I was all right. Eventually, my parents would drive the drive from Illinois to New York to retrieve their child. They had had enough of my New York escapades and wanted me to come home and live a normal life. They did not want to worry anymore. I no longer had any right to worry them. I became even more lost in New York. I didn't know if I was coming or going. I was not making the right decisions the right choices. So when they arrived, although came judgment as well, I was more than ready to return home.

I had interactions with men but I don't think I was ever taught how to date, who to date, or even why I should date.This scar, this skeleton in my closet made it difficult to trust any man that attempted to pursue me. I immediately assumed he had seen the videos or heard I was easy, so I played the game cautiously. I failed with every new player.

Me with all of my new found personalities, we all failed when it came to dating. I looked to each man as if he was the one. I gave any man a chance if he made the right first moves. I tried to make myself believe the things they'd tell me instead of always being defensive and a skeptic. It would have been a big relief to have been wrong. But I wasn't. I was never wrong.

Wounds take time to heal, sometimes it takes longer than expected. In my defense, no one prepared me for any of this. I wouldn't allow them to, even if they tried. Still, no one ever did prepare me for this. As if preparation for life would have made any of my decisions less damaging or less painful. I felt every back-breaking mistake. I performed surgery on myself with no anesthesia as a result of the changes needed in my life.

Each time I morphed into a new version of myself, I'd have to teach myself about this new person I was now going to be. After something bad happens, I'd run to escape the aftermath. Just as I had run from my mother that day back in Chicago. I ran from my mother's house into the arms of the porn industry, then into my own arms because only I can see the real me now. I played with men's emotions so easily. I did this to get what I wanted, which wasn't much at the time. Anxiety and depression still at the forefront of who I really am, it's easy to play the role of damsel in distress. Men just eat that shit up. So, I let them and every-time, trouble was never too far away.

But after I got back it was like my father and I weren't friends anymore like I wasn't the little girl who boasted about his songs playing over the church speakers during service because his mics were not hooked up right and he was playing secular music. I was the one who hung on his every word, who wanted to be like him, wanted to make him proud. And once again I was returning a failure and I had no clue what I would do next. I could tell that he was disappointed in me.

Officer Schwartz thanked me for being so candid with him. For allowing him to understand my relationship with my father, my relationship with myself and with men. I thanked him for allowing me a moment to vent. To explore how we got to this moment as I always needed to do.

"It sounds like you're dealing with a lot Rochelle." Said Officer Schwartz. "I think you should go and talk to someone and it's not something you have to figure out on your own I can have it done for you right now, if you like." He said.

looking down at my hands, I realized they were shaking and filled with sweat. Inside I felt like I'd explode or I had already exploded. It was obvious that I could no longer deal with my own emotions anymore and yes, the thought has crossed my mind, that, maybe I had met my match. "Will you make sure Roan is okay?" I asked him.

"Of course we will Rochelle. You don't have to worry about that. Worry about you. Let us worry about Roan." He said.

With a push of a button on the side of his walkie-talkie, he radioed in a code that brought the ambulance around the corner. They didn't allow me to go back in and I didn't try to. I allowed them to usher my arms to the waiting paramedics so that they could carry me the rest of the way. Exhausted from fighting so long, and losing so big, as my body met the stretcher, I let out a heavy sigh.

Healing Girls

After the ambulance arrived at the hospital and I was placed in a room with several police officers and staff members, my belongings were removed and put away for safety, by one of the nurses.

"Rochelle do you know what day it is?" Asked the social worker.

"Yes, I know the day." I responded.

"Do you know where you are?" she asked.

"In the nut house." I replied.

"Rochelle, what brought you here today?" she asked.

"I haven't been feeling myself lately." I said. " Nothing's been working out for me and lately, I've been more emotional than I'd like to be. I made a threat that I would end my life a few days ago and it's been a downward spiral ever since." I finished.

"Thank you for being so honest with me." She said.

"As opposed to what?" I asked.

"As opposed to hiding your feelings and not being honest." She fired back.

"Oh, I see you're quick on your feet." I responded.

"I like you a lot." She said. "We're going to have to ask you a few questions and get to know you a little bit, I hope that's okay." She said.

"That's fine with me. I don't mind." I said.

As she began to ask the questions and make queries into moments in my life the tears began to flow. I couldn't hold my head up and my shoulders were hunched over making it hard for me to breathe. Couldn't compose myself any longer. All of the pretending had caught up with me. I was fully into this nervous breakdown.

Administration and nurses began moving about making phone calls and asking questions about insurance and medications that I possibly take. There was so much going on so much commotion but yet the moment is still clear in my mind. Frozen in time, I sat there in a trance people moved about but I was not feeling included at all. As people began to come and go, in and out of the room, it became more and more quiet. Eventually it was only me in the room alone while the officer stood guard still outside.

As I glanced in-between the tears still sitting inside my eyes, I saw a dark-skinned woman wearing scrubs enter the room.

"Are you okay?" She asked. "You don't look okay." She said. "I'm Claudia and if you need anything I'll be right here." She said.

Seeing another Brown face in the sea of pale skin that was our everyday story-line, made me more aware of who I was and where I was and who I needed to pretend to be.

"Do you mind if I just sit here and talk to you if you need someone to talk to?" asked Claudia.

I looked over in her Direction but I didn't make eye contact. I gave her a nod and assured her that it would be okay if she stayed for a while. She took a seat and began to sit with her chair against the wall. One of the other nurses walked into the room holding a clipboard and began to ramble off questions, one after another.

"I need to get your work history." She said. "Can you start with your career or place of employment at the age of 20?" She asked.

"Well," I said, "that depends on how much about me you really want to know." Half smiling, I brushed back the tears and set up on the gurney. "There's this one time I was a stripper while working as a desk clerk at a hotel and going to Community College at the same time and doing a work-study program because my parents had unrealistic expectations. Is that where you want to start?" I asked.

"Wait a minute now." She said. "So you were stripping and going to college?" She asked.

We all laughed uncomfortably. After a few more questions the nurse left and it was just Claudia and I, sitting in the room.

"So tell me a little bit more about this stripping and Community College Rochelle." Said Claudia.

"I don't think I'm prepared to do this with you, right now." I told her.

"We have a little time before they transfer you to where you're going to be for a couple days ,if you want me to be honest." She said. "They're going to do a 7-Day hold on you. I just want you to know so you don't freak out when they come and tell you." She said.

I began to cry like a child who was wet and hungry.

"So tell me," she said, "tell me what I should know."

"Fine," I said, "fine. Maybe it'll help get my mind off of what's about to happen to me." I said.

* * *

"Comfortable in any road that I had taken up until that point, I returned from New York with my parents driving behind me in their PT Cruiser. Once I had returned to that small little town, with their small ideas full of prudery, I knew I couldn't stay there. I knew I had to find another way to escape. To escape my mom and to escape all of the nosy neighbors who knew nothing but thought they knew everything about my life. I didn't want to have to face those people. Who all knew that I had made mistakes. And had the evidence to prove it.

I still had big dreams and wanted to pursue College. But I figured I'd have to go the route that my mother had told me before I went to Tuskegee, that I would need to go to Community College. I didn't have any money to pay for it. And no one in my corner pushing me in the right direction or showing me which way to go. So like usual, I found all the information I could on what road I thought I wanted to go in. I'd make it out of this town. I'd make it to a University. I'd find a way to pay for it.

So I kept dancing. I didn't tell anyone. I would escape in the dead of night and return in the morning. I told them I worked overnight at a hotel. But I worked the day shift at the hotel and went to classes when I could. And I worked my work study at the community college.

Eventually I met someone at the club who knew someone at the university that I wanted to attend. He got me in contact with the financial aid office and helped me secure my acceptance at Howard University. I didn't really have a way to get there. My car wasn't working anymore and I didn't have any money and like always my parents supported me from afar. One of the guys who was at the club on a couple of occasions would come home from Hampton University and visit where I danced. The semester that I was to begin my studies, he gave me a ride to the campus from Illinois and I gave him one in return.

Howard was a great experience. It was everything I've ever wanted it to be. I learned more about African American studies than I could have ever dreamed. I met some intelligent people. Only a few people brought up my past. There were only a few times where I felt like an outcast. I still didn't have direction. I was easily overwhelmed and with little to no financial support backing me, when one of our classmates committed suicide out of one of the dormitory windows because she was gay and her family didn't accept her, I decided to leave and once again, I returned home to my parents.

When I returned home it was clear that my parents wanted me to get a job and to get a job right away. I was exploring my sexuality, something I never thought I'd do. I was enjoying it and I no longer wanted to date men. I was a flirt with women but never took anything seriously. But after my classmate's suicide, I thought it would be desecrating her memory if I didn't pursue how I really felt inside.

That summer when I returned from Howard, I took up a job working at a bank call center in the fraud department, a few doors down from my mother's Department. Since I was now home and trying to work a normal nine-to-five to save some money to repair all of the credit that I had destroyed over the years trying to pursue a dream, I tried to fully embrace the notion of being normal. I desperately wanted a relationship.

Having meaningful honest relationships are foreign to me. Even now. I started searching for a relationship similar to that of my parents. This was an impossible task. They met unintentionally and grew up together. They are still growing together. I wanted someone to call my own, to validate me, to prove to myself that I was not damaged and that I was worth someone loving. We met in July, at work and her name was Kendall.

I didn't hang around many people. There were a few people that I talked to at work. It had been a few years since my internet scandal and I was less guarded. The past few years had offered a glimpse into who I was meant to be as a Black girl. Although it offered no guidance on what direction I should go in my life.

She was beautiful, goofy, unsure of herself, but somehow still commanded my attention. I had no clue how I was going to make a move on her. We didn't work in the same department and only saw each other in passing but every time I saw her, I lit up like a Christmas tree. She brought out this side of me that I longed to feel comfortable putting on display. I wanted her to notice me.

I followed her. This was the first time that I felt like this. There was an unbearable force pulling me towards her. There were no red flags that warned me to stay away. I saw no signs of baby mama drama, I saw no signs of abuse, and no signs she wouldn't be able to hold an interesting conversation. I pulled my co-worker to the side and asked her to stake out her car with me after work. I was too embarrassed to do this alone and I needed support.

We waited in the car until Kendall walked out of the office. She was the definition of fine. I never looked at women and fell in love by how they appealed to me physically, but how they looked at me. She looked at me like she could see right into me and she would always smile. We watched as she walked to her car and drove off. That was all I needed to know. For a week I placed a rose on her car windshield every day. I didn't tell her it was me, I really wanted her to feel loved and special. I wanted her to feel valued.

I saw her in the halls a few times after that. She finally asked my name after referring to me by the university name written on my sweatshirt for a few weeks.

We started talking. For once I had no expectations and no written script. I was playing it by ear, finally, living a life. There was no real courtship, not like I was told it should be. I don't think either one of us knew how to date or the purpose behind dating. My parents were kids when they met and their families were instrumental in the survival of their courtship. We had no such luxury.

I was still trying to satisfy people around me, my family. I remained in character with everyone but Kendall. With Kendall, I was myself. We spent all of our time together, shopping, eating, laughing, trusting one another with the under surface sections of our lives we granted each other admittance to. I was too young and naive to really understand and appreciate what she offered. I loved her hard, unintentionally, yet still on purpose.

As we spent more time together I began to fight with myself, not knowing which me to give her. I wanted to be cautious because I felt myself slipping into unfamiliar territory. I wanted her to like me for who I was but I was broken and I didn't even know who that was. I never stopped to assess the damages from previous mistakes. I kept all of this inside, of course, I felt emotions but never expressed them and I never shared them. I learned from my past, not to be so open. I initially gave my true self unapologetically. She noticed my change, it was impossible to conceal. I tried to be her doll, be what she needed me to be when she needed me to be it.

She said things like, "you're too good for me," "you're going to be great one day," and "I don't want to hold you back from what you're supposed to do in this world." I didn't fight her when she told me these things because I believed she believed in what she was saying. Love is crazy like that. I eventually realized that I was a Black girl that would fall in love with anything and anyone that put forth any amount of effort to get to know me. I wasn't battling as many self-confidence issues but I was a lonely girl. I had little to no standards when it came to the people I'd give myself to. I was starving for a personal connection and intimacy. I would take it from whomever offered it.

My relationships after Kendall were filled with emotional and physical abuse. I tried to look for love. I didn't have the patience to wait for love to find me. I was doing some exploring and trying to figure myself out for the umpteenth time. During my brief stint in college I played with the idea of dating women but I never really took it seriously. After Kendall, I wanted something different. I wanted to feel a different way, to be treated a different way, and to be seen a different way.

I placed myself in danger looking for love.

That's when I met Remy. One night on a down low website, I was checking profiles, commenting on flash messages, and chatting in the rooms, as usual. Gay women were hidden so you would always need to search for them. She was cute, adorable. She looked like a little Hispanic boy. She was from Detroit but was living in Texas. Our very first conversation was an argument over religion. She must've thought I was going to back down or something but intellect wouldn't allow my defeat. She was turned on and we began using our mushy voices towards one another almost immediately.

She was 12 years older but she was the type to make plans and to make you feel secure and unafraid. She reassured my every doubt. Within a month of knowing one another, online only, I was on my way to the airport to have a same day wedding in Texas.

Working in the same office with my mom and living back at home now older had given us the chance to try to mend our relationship as mother and daughter. Although she preferred for me to keep my lifestyle a secret, because she was more in the closet then I was, I still felt the need to leave and find my own way.

The day that she dropped me off in front of the airport I heard her voice trembled as she hugged me. Struggling trying to find her words and force them out, all while trying not to shed a tear, she adjusted her eyeglasses. Fixing her floral blouse and zipping her sweat suit jacket she hugged me again as I said goodbye and disappeared into Chicago's O'Hare Airport.

When I returned from college my sister made a big deal about her disapproving of my sexual orientation. She felt like I needed to be more of a big sister. More of a role model. I shook my head when she said this. I thought to myself, who was a role model for me?"

"So you just upped and went to Texas?" Said Claudia.

"Yes, I upped and went to Texas." I replied.

"When we first met online, she told me everything I needed to hear. I was a sucker for love. A hopeless romantic. I believed that people were innately good. My insecurities exposed, I opened up to her. We did what was called uhauling, in the lesbian community. After our simple civil ceremony with vows we wrote and exchanged and a cake with a rainbow and champagne, I met her friends and we enjoyed each other's company.

Afterwards we cuddled in bed and embraced each other watching television. She began to fall asleep when I was startled by the sound of my cellular phone. I crept down the stairs to answer as the number was from my college ex boyfriend. We still kept in contact because he was a good man and also a good friend. Sometimes he called just to tell me about his day and to check on me. As we giggled on the phone and talked about the happenings back at Howard, where he was still enrolled in a doctoral program, I heard the sound of footsteps, as Remy made her way down to the lower level.

She walked over to me and stood over me with her fists balled. I looked up at her and told her, "One moment." As I gestured with my finger. Within seconds I could feel her fist barreling towards me with the speed of light. Startled and afraid I sat there in a daze as I took stock of the fact that my wife had just punched me in the face and knocked the phone out of my hands. She began to beat on me. To pound on me. I fought her off. I fought back. Some swings were stronger than others. I was caught off guard. I was fighting for my life. We fought all night long. Going back and forth. An obvious power struggle. I packed my shit and grabbed everything I could. At the first sign of sunlight, the next day oh, I made my way, stiletto heels and all, down the cracked sidewalk walking, toward the nearest hotel.

I found a cheap hotel down the road and called my mother. She immediately made arrangements to wire transfer me some money so I could leave. I left the hotel once I checked in so I could grab some food and figure out my surroundings. Once I returned to the room, my key was no longer working to the room door. I made my way downstairs to the desk and asked the clerk, what the problem was.

He looked at me and said, "Ma'am your wife has already canceled your room and she's waiting for you."

Just as he finished his statement I felt a brush of hot air on my right shoulder. It was Remy. She was standing there staring me down. She asked me to go to the elevator and walked me up to the room. She told me to get my things that I had placed on the floor in front of the door and bring them down the stairs. I followed her directions and got into her car.

After we returned home she apologized for causing such a scene and for physically assaulting me. She stated that she loved me and didn't want to be with anyone else. That she didn't want anyone else to have me. She was apologetic about being jealous. I believed her and wanted to give her another chance because I couldn't allow this to fail. This went on for a few weeks she and I, arguing about small things, fighting about big things, finding out lies that she told. Her real age and the fact that she had an adult son. It was almost too much to bear but I gritted and I grinned in order to try to make this a successful marriage-a successful partnership.

She wasn't working, she was taking classes at TSU. I hadn't found a new job since I left my job back in Illinois. I took up sex call operator positions and decided to take a couple of adult photos to put food on the table for nights when we had nothing to eat. One night in February, I made a connection with one of the photographers that I worked with back in New York. It turned out that he was in Texas and he wanted to shoot me for a few scenes. I agreed to meet him at a local motel so I could make a couple extra dollars.

Remy found out and when I returned she was waiting for me at the door. She began to punch me in my face until I fell. She had Timberland boots on so she kicked me in my stomach with them over and over again. She pulled me by my hair and dragged me down the sidewalk in front of all the neighbors. She stomped on my face and stomped me into the ground over and over and no one helped. They just looked on as I lay there in the parking lot of our complex. After this, I went back inside. I locked myself in the bathroom and I didn't come out until the next day. I made a plan in my head to get away. I knew that the only thing she was going to do was kill me and I wasn't going to stay to let it happen.

Still going on with the plan and making her believe that I was happy to still be there, I was cooking and cleaning and making life easier for me and for her. I was looking for jobs and had found one working at the same company the same bank my mother and I had worked for back in Illinois. I was talking to my mother and my grandmother more on the phone. I was missing home and wanted someone close to me. I would walk to the nearest gym or grocery store just to get time alone to speak with them. I would periodically walk to the grocery store although Remy had a car. It was a stick shift and I didn't know how to drive a stick shift.

This particular February morning, when I wanted to make chili, I told my mom to give me the list of ingredients in the recipe and I would go to the store and pick up the items so that I could make it later that day. It was 9 a.m. and I was walking alone and I enjoyed the walk as I normally did. I was on the phone with my friend back at home her name was Joy and she was a Joy to talk to. While in the grocery store I was carrying a basket in my arms. something came over me and I felt as if hands were over my shoulders pressing me down into the floor. I told Joy I need to call her back later. I hung up the phone, placed the grocery cart on the floor in the middle of the aisle, and made my way out of the front door as I didn't want to faint in front of anyone.

I put my jacket down on the concrete outside of the grocery store right behind one of the pillars of the building. I placed a phone call to Remy to let her know that I didn't feel well and that something was going on. As I laid my back down on the jacket that was on the ground, I placed my feet in the air because something just told me to elevate my legs.

The security guard circling the parking lot pulled over and instructed me that, "ma'am you cannot lay here."

I threw my phone at him as I had dialed nine-one-one and told him to, "tell them where I am." There were people standing all around me now. My eyes were blurry and I felt like I was slowly fading away. I felt as if I was losing myself but I didn't know why. The ambulance arrived and they loaded me into the back. They begin to ask me questions. They asked my name, my age, where I was from, what pills I had taken that day, and what drugs I was on.

I was pissed. "How dare you assume that I'm a drug addict just because I'm on the ground at 9 a.m. in the morning outside of grocery store. I make more than all of you guys put together." I told them. We arrived at the hospital and they begin to walk the gurney in while instructing the triage team that, "she was just speaking fine in the ambulance, a moment ago."

As I began to panic because I could feel myself slipping away, I asked them to, "move my arms, move my left arm because I can't feel it and I can't feel me breathing."

One doctor yelled over at me, "you're talking so you're breathing."

I told him with the look of fear in my eyes, "I cannot feel myself breathing." At this moment there's a foul smell in the air that is now dancing across everyone's nose. I can smell it. And they can smell it too. everything that is in my body has now exited my body. As the triage team realizes what is happening, my eyes begin to roll in the back of my head, they begin to roll the stretcher down the hall into the operating room. I can feel tugs on my clothing as they begin to cut away the material to expose my body.

I woke up a few hours later. Remy and one of her friends were sitting in the room next to me. The doctor said that they don't know what it was and they're going to still have to do more tests. I told him that I felt fine, that I could go. The doctor bet that if I could walk from the gurney to the bed, in the room that they were trying to keep me in, then I could go home. I agreed to the bet. As I tried to lift my body from the wheelchair into the bed in the room I again lost all bodily functions. I couldn't walk. I didn't know it but I could no longer walk. I was placed in the hospital where they ran tests and they screened me from everything from lupus to cancer to HIV. The conclusion, "transverse myelitis. Inflammation of the spinal cord. There is no cure. You may never walk again. You'll be here in this hospital and someone call her mom," they said.

I stayed in the hospital for a few weeks. I was determined to walk again. You couldn't keep me down. So seven days later, I was doing stairs in the hallway at the hospital. They had no choice but to send me home. Back to Remy. But while I was in the hospital, she and I had already argued over me ordering room service and forgetting to order her tray. To her concern of having to possibly care for me for the rest of my crippled life. She made my Hospital stay more about her than she did about me. I realized that I desperately needed to go.

Once released from the hospital I was put on several medications. My parents hadn't arrived yet but I heard that they were on their way to Texas. By the time they got there, I was already drugged and high. Remy had been feeding me all of the pills that the doctor had prescribed. One after 1 after 1. I was becoming addicted. I lived like a zombie. I was learning to walk fully again. Without the assistance of a walker. She took full advantage. full advantage of my handicap.

When my parents arrived I didn't want them to see the type of horror and hell that I was living in and had signed up for. They saw right through her, I tried to hide the wounds on my body. I tried to hide the sadness in my eyes. I think they knew that I was being controlled and that I needed them I just couldn't tell them. They begged for me to return back to Illinois with them but I told them that I wouldn't. So when they left my mother made a promise to return as often as she could to make sure I was okay.

For the next few months she delivered on that promise. She got her same position in Texas as she had an Illinois with the same company just to come and make sure I was recovering okay. She would come down every other weekend to work at that office and then return home and work her normal shift. It even gave me an opportunity to return to work as I went in as a member of her department. I continued to try to make it work with Remy but after suicide attempts on her behalf, multiple encounters with physical abuse, I was ready for an escape plan. My mother sent money so that I could leave and I hopped on a train and left.

I wasn't fully recovered when I returned to Illinois but my mother did everything she could to find me a neurologist, get me the right diagnosis, and make sure that I had the right care team. She really stepped up and was a true soldier but like always I couldn't sit still. I got a job working at her department and my ideas and creativity began to come out of me. I wanted to make more money and I wanted to enjoy what I did. Remy and I were still going back and forth. She had moved up to Illinois and said she wasn't going to let me go. She had been to jail, found a sugar daddy, and became more of a fem than I ever was. My mom said that she looked like my twin. She and I tried to make it work as I made my way up the ranks at the new job. We wanted two different things, two different lifestyles and two different definitions of love.

During Pride weekend I met a stud from Chicago that really piqued my interest and help me get over Remy. She was Remy's complete opposite. She could do no wrong and she would never hurt a fly. I was fresh out of a domestic violence relationship and I shouldn't have been dating at all. I know I hurt her and so I had to leave the relationship before I hurt her anymore. I made my way through women over the years going back and forth between Remy and Kendall and added a couple of more in there. For some reason, I wasn't secure in my decision to solely date women and wanted to give traditional relationships a try again. I actually wanted a child so I ended my relationship with a woman I was dating so that I could try to have a child of my own.

I contacted a few of my male friends that I've known over the years and one of them agreed to be a donor for me to conceive a child. During the process we tried to make a traditional relationship work but I was selfish and that's not what I wanted at the time so I left him to have a child on my own."

"Wait, so you're telling me that after everything you went through Rochelle, you decided to have a kid on your own?" Claudia asked.

"Yeah I can't really tell you what I was thinking." I said. "My logic was I didn't want to reach the age of 30 and be single and not have a kid so I figured I'd get one out of the way.

My family was on board and I never really thought about how I was letting go of the life I'd finally started to grow accustomed to even if it was just for a little bit. I moved from the city back into my parents' house with my little sister. I was laid off from my bank job where I had worked my way up to the project management office downtown Chicago. I was making about $30 an hour before they laid me off and I was having fun and the time of my life. When I left the city I also left the Asian woman that I was dating at the time. She was upset to say the least that I would decide to have a family on my own.

I was going to take this time to develop a relationship with my mother. We had grown closer over the years but still not close enough. I thought that she could help me raise this child and it would bond us for life. So I began to set up a nursery in their home and I shared my journey on social media to ease my loneliness. I didn't think about a job at this time or even planning the future for the child I was going to have. I was just simply going through the motions because this was something that I thought I should be doing at this age. I put up cribs and changing tables, I hung alphabets and decorations on the walls. I searched online for love and found myself calling on old flames to ease my pain.

My Asian ex would take me to doctor's appointments from time to time. And Kendall, my Ex from the summer after college, she was away in the military in Italy but she would return mid-pregnancy for a surgery of her own. I traveled to visit her and to take care of her as much as I could as she recovered from her procedure. We made plans to be together and to raise the baby together but for some reason distance had altered our course.

I was starting to worry that I would be raising this baby really alone. The questions from doctors and acquaintances , 'where is the dad?' were beginning to weigh on me. I wasn't certain if I wanted to have a man or a woman raise the child with me and I wasn't sure that it mattered but I saw the nasty looks when I was dating women and I wasn't certain that I wanted the same looks while leading my child through this adult playground .

It was Mother's Day 2010. I was in full-blown labor and lying in the hospital bed. I had only recently learned as I checked myself into the hospital that I wouldn't be able to have an epidural, due to my spinal condition. Through agony and pain I replied to text messages and social media posts congratulating me on this Mother's Day.

Lonely, tired and partially panicked I responded to a Happy Mother's Day text message from an old friend from one of my lesbian social groups. Her name was Fila. She was from Detroit but she was in Illinois working with one of the big motor companies. We hung out at the club a couple times. She was more like a stud and into really fem girls so we just clicked. While in labor I responded to her message and said, "thank you we almost have a baby."

She immediately picked up the phone and called me. "We almost have a baby?" she asked.

"Yes, we almost have a baby." I told her.

She sat on the phone with me as I was in labor and endured every scream as the contractions came and went. We bonded over my pain and over her telling me and reminding me to breathe. Once Roan had arrived, I made an announcement that solidified our bond.

"We have a boy." I said. She was so excited and couldn't hold back her joy.

"I want to cry." She said. "Me too" I said. We carried on like that all night long and into the early morning. Roan and I had to stay in the hospital for the next few days because he came out jaundiced. Fila remained on the phone with me and assured me that everything would be okay once I returned home.

My younger sister had recently told the family that she was now pregnant. Six years her senior, I felt it was unfair that she would be procreating at the same time that I was. This was my time with my parents for them to guide me. As soon as she told us I felt the need to move. To give them their space so they could help their youngest child bring her child into this world. I felt she needed them more than I did.

Talking on the phone to Fila for those days and confiding in her she told me that she'd be there for me and that I didn't have to do it alone. She told me what I wanted to hear. And it was music to my ears. It was the next day after we returned from the hospital when she picked Roan and I up and drove us out to Rockford where she resided.

Sitting on the porch when we arrived to her beautiful home was a tall box. When we got inside and opened it up I pulled out a life-size bear with the same theme that I had chosen for Roan's Nursery. It was a beautiful gesture and just what I needed. We went out shopping for Roan. We purchased all of those cute things that I always wanted to purchase but had no one to go to the store with me. We got cute outfits and laughed and joked about things together. We talked about past relationships and abuse in relationships and how we didn't think that abuse was okay. We settled into a routine even going as far as to take family portraits when Roan was just six weeks.

During this time, Fila was going back and forth to Detroit to visit her friends and family. I was staying with my parents. We talked on the phone day and night. We wanted the same things. I was at her house every day, almost , after she returned. I noticed that her ex girlfriend was texting and calling her constantly. I had learned not to create something out of nothing with Fila but I wasn't about to be played. I was dealing with postpartum pain & undiagnosed depression. The doctor prescribed a painkiller with codeine in it. Lots of codeine. I didn't know it at the time but it was the same type of pills that Fila was trafficking. Once she found out that I had a script, she started controlling me with them. One time I got loud with her and she beat me to the ground. We'd end up married and in Detroit two years later with her still beating me into the ground and with Roan now showing signs of being delayed due to all the trauma he was witnessing.

I was fully strung out. I had gone from a fearful new mother to an opiod head hearing voices coming from the attic of her closet. Its true. I actually walked my mom and sister into me and Fila's closet one day and asked them to be quiet so they could hear the voices. I was taking seizure pills, pain pills, and sleeping pills all at one time. Anything I could do to escape the hell of a world I had designed for myself. I eventually found my way back into Information Technology and Project Management for a major automotive company in Detroit. We had been living out of a roach motel and the only working vehicle we had was my 2005 cobalt.

Fila finally secured a small house for us to rent from her cousin's baby daddy. It was in the hood but I didn't care. It wasn't long before she started beating me in that house too. I called the police on her and had her arrested but I dropped the charges when her family became upset with me. They were all I had in Detroit. They weren't a rescue squad but in case of emergency, I needed them as much on my side as possible. Right before Roan turned 2, I took some pills I got from her brother and almost died. I had to beg them to release me from the hospital in time enough for his birthday party. It was the day before the party and my parents were due in town the next morning.

My father wasted no time telling me how he didn't raise me to live in a neighborhood like this and how I was too skinny. They would leave and it would be six months before I could finally escape Fila and flee Detroit for good.

"So you and Roan escaped?" Asked Claudia.

"Yes, it took a lot but I needed to get him into a safe environment."

"Oh my god," she said. "I wish I could hear more but I think your transport is here," she said. "Is it okay if I give you a hug?" She asked.

"Yes it's okay."

"Listen," I said. "Since we can't continue this bonding moment during my emotional meltdown, I'll tell you this," I said. "Eventually, I gave up. Gave up on love, on living, on accomplishing anything. It was just easier to do nothing, to desire nothing. It was less responsibilities and fewer emotions I'd be forced to feel. I've allowed my fear, depression, and anxiety to speak for me for far too long. They control every relationship I have. Some prey on the weak. Its as if they can see me coming before I even begin my journey in their direction. I'm sick and tired of pretending to have it all together."

"Look," said Claudia. "No one has it all together. Don't you worry. You'll get fixed up when it's your time. Just don't stop fighting." She told me as she bent towards me to place my belongings on the bed. Patting my purse, she winked and said, "Your Journey is just beginning home girl. See you later."

Interrupted Girls

I had to be woken up when we arrived to the hospital. It had been days since the fight with my father and I was exhausted being transported from the emergency room where they completed my intake and transferred me to the Community Hospital, where the extra security measures and guards made it feel more like a prison. They immediately inspected my belongings for my safety and the safety of the staff. They made me remove my shoes and all clothing items. They made me shower and use a non sulfate free shampoo on my hair to make sure I didn't have lice. They gave me a uniform and hospital socks, handed me a toothbrush and a travel-size toothpaste and a bar of soap. They gave me my documents and began to Rattle off a list of medication that the doctor had recommended.

"Gabapentin 100 milligrams, one to three times daily. Paroxetine 10 mg one daily. Oxcarbazepin 300mg every 12 hours." They read off my diagnosis depression, anxiety, mild OCD. They led me to a common area and showed me the activities and snacks that were available. There were other patients on the ward in the common area with me.

I was told that I would meet the social worker tomorrow and that my schedule would be provided in the morning. I was asked many questions about my health and mental status at that moment. I didn't know how to feel. I wanted my son. I wanted to leave. I began to talk to the other inmates slash prisoners. There were people talking to themselves in the corner and people using the courtesy phones on the wall. There were girls coloring and there were people watching Ellen on TV. I gazed off into space. Keeping my thoughts inside. Deep down I wanted to cry. But I couldn't let anyone see me weak.

Once they placed me in my room, I realized I had a roommate. She was and almond skinned, big brown-eyed, Indian girl who tried to kill herself. She told me that her husband had committed her and she didn't know what she would do. I felt bad for her. I began to talk to her more because I didn't want her to feel alone. We talked about our childhoods. We talked about how life wasn't what we thought it was going to be. She didn't seem mentally unstable to me. She just seemed sad.

"What ended you up in here?" She asked

"I think what really ended me in here," I said, "was my many failed relationships, my many attempts on love and becoming addicted to any and everything I possibly could. After I left Fila and we were still married but I left her still, I returned to a familiar face. A woman that I had been seeing off and on whenever Fila and I had problems. She had become a part of Roan's life. She was helping to stabilize mine. I used her. I used her kindness. I used her financial support. I used her energy. All she wanted was to feel loved and to be loved and to be able to give love and I knew that and I took advantage of it. As I tried to wean myself off of Narcotics, off of the pills, off of the bad relationships, I stayed under her. I allowed her to protect me and I allowed her to protect Roan and although she was in it for a relationship, a family, I on the other hand, did not have that same goal in mind.

So eventually I would get clean. I would stop taking pills. I would begin a business venture, an events and Conference child care company. I was very good at it and at the same time I returned to the IT project management field. I was driving 3 hours to work in Wisconsin for a $90,000 contract daily with my son and I was trying to push a business as well and it was becoming overwhelming. So as I started to push the business I met a man by the name of Arnold who I was able to talk to and who cared about my well-being.

He was the first man in almost 10 years that I had really given time and attention to. He's the first man that I had allowed to be in my son's life. So I left the woman's house who had rescued me. And Roan and I went to Wisconsin where we stayed in a hotel until I was able to finish my IT contract. Once I completed my IT contract, my relationship with Arnold was going well. I decided to leave Wisconsin since I had nowhere to go and I was running out of money. Roan and I drove from Wisconsin to Tennessee where we would stay with Arnold.

I didn't adjust to the lifestyle right away. As much as I wanted a two-parent home for my son I wasn't sure that Arnold was the right one. He made it very clear that he did not intend for us to stay with him. I lied and told him I was going to find a place but the truth was I had nowhere to go. His mother had just moved in with him and she did not know me from Adam or Eve. She didn't like me either. I tried to make them adjust to life with me and Roan. I eventually found my way in the IT world of Nashville. I began to contract for major Fortune 500 companies.

The culture in the company's was mostly the same as the Midwest or the North. I was usually the only black woman in the office and the youngest. I could never get a good groove going at any one of the companies. It was like something was always off. I was always anxious. I always felt alone. Unappreciated. It's like I had these positions and no one knew what the role really was. I became more and more depressed even in Nashville. My pills replaced with alcohol I began to lash out at Arnold. Every little thing that he did drove me insane. He hummed, I wanted to slit his throat." I said, as I looked over at my roommate. "My bad." I said. "But you know what I mean."

She nodded.

"We began to argue about every little thing and sleeping separately. He was only letting me hang around because of the kid and I used that to my advantage. He told Roan, from the beginning, that he would remain in his life no matter what. The clock was ticking on our time together.I was still working until one afternoon, I walked past a TV in our office and it was showing a news broadcast of a sorority girl found dead in a Texas jail cell. As I watched the broadcast, I moved closer and closer to the screen. The girl's face was familiar. As soon as it clicked, I went to her social media and my worst fears were brought to light.

We had grown up in the same church, sung in the same choir, both praise danced, and I had always admired how she and her sisters were a united front. If you fought one you had to fight all five of them. I could barely drive home after work. My eyes were blurry and tears were steady. I had just recently commented on one of her videos and told her to be careful. I knew that woke activists become targets and I didn't want her to be in that number. I couldn't accept that she had taken her own life. I knew better.

I signed for a new truck and left my six figure job so I could drive back to Illinois and help sing my sister to rest. Our church was a community within a community. We had become young adults together and now here we were again, many of us home only to bury our dear sister. It was confirmed that I was no longer employed once I had broken down in the middle of a meeting and once I returned from the funeral. This only led me into a deeper depression. My relationship on the rocks, I lashed out at Arnold more and more each day until we both finally snapped and it was time for me to leave. He was too good of a man to ever put his hands on me.

I started talking to men online and hooking up with old flames. Roan and I lived out of a hotel for almost a month before we stayed with my former co-worker and her boyfriend. She was a younger sistah but I had given her my cobalt so she could get back and forth to work, after I purchased my truck, so we were cool. Roan and I eventually left after she accused me of wanting to make a white chocolate swirl with her man. We found another hotel and used the points from our last hotel stay to crash for a few more weeks. Around Halloween, we loaded up the cobalt and headed back to Illinois. We lost the truck after a head on collision. I had insurance and was waiting on a 10,000 dollar settlement. I was going to use the money to start over.

Even before we could arrive in Illinois I had begun flirting with a man online who was a member of my brother fraternity. His name isn't relevant but I can tell you that he's the only reason I actually put one foot in front of the other and decided to start driving home. He gave me something to look forward to because I obviously hadn't had enough of life's adventures.

We would sit on the phone all night, he and I, when I was still in Nashville. He gave me hope. Made me feel like there was a possibility that at the end of all this, I would be happy. The thought of him made me excited about what tomorrow would bring. He had daughters and was married. But he was on the verge of divorce he just needed to get the money together to pay his attorney. He was in the military and looked good in a uniform. He made promises that he'd be there, in Illinois, when I arrived.

We began spending time together when I arrived to Illinois and as I began to settle into my parents home again with Roan, he began to spend the night here or there. Much like most of us over the age of 30 he would indulge in alcohol. A beverage here and a beverage there. I didn't think much of it. Being in the military and an alcoholic was just a mix. Over the weeks I would be sick with a cold or he'd be hungover. Our attitudes both worsened. It didn't make it any easier that one night while staying over, he walked around my mother's house with only his underwear on. My father was appalled. Luckily I didn't get kicked out but they let me know that he was not as welcomed as he thought he was.

It was time for him to pay his attorney and he did not have the funds. He asked if I could help and I told him I would do it with no problem. I had just received my settlement from my accident and I was rolling in dough. I gave him the money for his divorce and took him and his girls out for a weekend getaway, all-expenses-paid. A few weeks later he stopped returning my phone calls and distanced himself for me. It was clear that he had no plans for a future with me. I don't think I felt something when he told me. I know I acted as if I felt something. I know I lashed out. I know I stalked him and stalked his location for quite some time afterwards. But I don't think I felt anything. I had already become numb. Just hadn't realized it yet.

"I'm sorry you had to go through all of that Rochelle." Said my roommate. I hadn't even had time to ask her name as I had begun confessing my life's woes. I asked her if she was okay. And she said that she was.

As the doors begin to lock and I began to take stock that we were locked inside the hospital, the only noise I could hear was the sound of the clock hand moving and the sound of my roommate breathing quietly 2 feet away.

"Do you want to know something funny?" I ask her. "Right after I paid for his divorce and he left me, he married somebody else. Isn't that Karma for you?" I asked.

"So I guess we're locked in here for the night and we can't move the furniture because it's all tacked down to the floor, so I guess this is it roomie." I said

"What did you do?" She asked. "How did you get over it?"

"I can't say that there was anything to really get over." I said. "I took stock in myself. I realized that there was something about me that was attracting these type of people in my life. I realize that there are changes that I need to make in my own insecurities that no one other human being could help me with. So I got in the mirror. I knew that I wore weaves and makeup because I didn't like my outer appearance. I asked myself is this something that I could change is this something that I control and I made a decision. I gave myself an answer. I could grow my hair. I had to at least attempt to before I went back to ever wearing synthetic hair, someone else's hair. I can at least try to resolve my own issues. I could fix my skin and learn to love the lights and lows of my face and to sleep well and eat well. I could make the attempt to allow myself the opportunity to be seen the way that I felt I should have been seen. I had to learn how to value myself before I could require anyone else value me." I finished.

"So did you do this? Are you happy with yourself?" She asked

"I'm on the road. I'm on the journey. I just haven't arrived yet." I said.

I didn't sleep at all during the night. I tossed and turned and gazed off into the bright green light bouncing off the window. It was just high enough that the average person couldn't see out of it. Probably made that way to prevent us mentally disabled folks from trying to jump through it. It looked to be extra thick glass, so I wouldn't have recommended it anyway.

I pressed the intercom button to request one of the nurses let me out of my cage so I could make my approach to the nurses station. They took their time answering. My emergency was not their emergency. I requested something to help me sleep. Whatever they gave me, didn't work. So I lied there, all night. With my eyes directed at the ceiling but my mind in a totally different place.

When I heard the unlocking of the doors and as they began to slide open, we all began to file outside of our rooms, one by one. Each standing on their designated side of the wall as per staff. We were to stand in line and take the pills that were already set aside for us as they called our names. I had no clue what the hell it was that I was putting in my body. All that I could think was, don't swallow. The nurse would make you open your mouth, stick out your tongue, and move it all around to make sure you took the pills. We showered with four minutes each to complete the task. Afterward, the staff would explain the schedule for the day and lead us to the day-room to have breakfast. At least, their version of breakfast. All of the meals were more like prison food than hospital food and they didn't give you a choice.

Sitting next to me in the classroom like chairs, at the cafeteria like table, was my suicidal roommate. I was aware of my own mental status but she really worried me. I was concerned for her well-being. She had become attached to me within less than 24 hours. She lifted her fork when I lifted mine, she looked to me for approval before she did anything. I couldn't take advantage of her vulnerability but I could see how forming these types of attachments so quickly could land you in the nuthouse. She said her name was S. J. and I told her to call me Chelle. "My friends call me Chelle," I said, although they were few, far, and in between.

Seated across from us was a long and thin boy who said his name was Thomas. He apparently was the president and sole member of the welcoming committee. He had been here for over a week. He excitedly showed us to the arts & craft corner, the VHS movie collection, and the pile of graham crackers and apple juice sitting out for our snacking needs. It was at this moment that reality punched me in the gut. My focus switched from the flamboyant mental ward tour guide to the space I began to feel dividing my soul from my body. I could see myself standing there. I circled her, me. I glanced towards the door. I wanted to escape.

"Group meeting in room A in 5 minutes, everyone." Called one of the aids.

I hated group discussions or any form of group therapy. Just like high-school, I couldn't stand waiting around for someone to understand something that I already thought I knew. I was tempted to forego participating. I didn't want to get pulled in to any conversation where I'd actually have to put my intellect on display. I didn't want anyone to make a big deal about me speaking the way that I did or how much of a caring and understanding person I was. I wanted to fly under the radar but the person sitting next to me, on the left side, as SJ was on the right, captivated my attention and for their comfort level, I decided to play along.

I couldn't tell if the person sitting next to me was a male or female. Not that it mattered, but I wanted to know the correct adjectives to use when communicating with him or her, especially since this instructor, therapist, group leader, whatever they were called, was putting us in little groups and requiring that we talk to one another during the team building exercise. I didn't know how this would help me. I'm a grown woman, not a seventeen year old with emotional issues. I have real life problems that your team building exercise won't do anything but irritate me.

Bethany was their name. She looked more like a Henry or a Bellamy but she introduced herself as Bethany. I didn't pay it too much attention. I could tell that she was shy among us Sis gendered folks and I didn't want to give her any more reason to feel agitated. We were already in the nuthouse.

"What adjectives do you prefer?" I asked.

She looked at me like I had just opened a window in a stuffy room.

"I like they, them, you." She replied with her face lit up into a smile. "Thank you for asking me that." They said.

"Oh darling, it's not that big of a deal. I just wanted to make sure that I addressed a friend correctly." I told them.

They were young. Had to be in their twenties. White. Blonde, and would have been able to pass for successful white man, given the right training. I didn't judge. I knew that I had no clue about what was going on inside that head, what the cells were doing to that body, and how their environment had played a part in altering the code of the inhabitant of this particular vessel. As we sat in class and right before we let out to lunch, we all were distracted by a new inmate arriving in style. We could see him through the glass frame of the classroom. He was restrained in a wheelchair. His mouth was gagged and his hands were bound. They processed him as we walked to the day-room for lunch.

I could make my first phone call home. I didn't know what I was going to say. I was embarrassed. I felt weak. I was worried about Roan and I could barely focus with all of the medication they had me on. I raised the receiver and dialed the number with the outside line access code. My mother answered. Our conversation was short. A few how is its, and a few more "what you gone do with your life Chelle"'s later, and I was still alive. I wanted to speak with Roan but I was too afraid that the reminder that I was not there in the flesh would hurt him more than if he has put me out of his mind, for now.

The nurses, caught up in their own world with no regard for the humanity of their patients, jokingly heard us down the hall for our nightly lock in. Totally removed from the fact that each person here is having some type of battle, they make light of situations heavy enough to crush the Earth.

When we awake for day two, I'm back to feeling myself. I'm taking the meds but I'm watching closely as everything happens around me. On today's schedule is yoga and therapy. I knew the only way to make this time go faster was not to fight it. So I gave in and began to participate.

Our first class was led by a woman who looked to be afflicted with dwarfism and when she spoke you could tell that she was working with a severe lisp. I wasn't knocking her, but it was obvious that the other patients were not taking her seriously. I pulled out my mat and begin to stretch. The first person to join in, was my S.J.. She didn't hesitate, moving in stride and rhythm with my feet, she grabbed a mat and took her stance. We lunged forward with one leg, positioning our thighs parallel to the ground. Our feet pointing forward. our torsos facing forward in the direction of our lunge. We raised our arms upward to the sky and relaxed our shoulders, lift our rib-cage upward and gazed ahead.

"You're really into this." S.J. was looking in my direction now.

"What the Warrior One position?" I asked, repeating the name the instructor had just told the class. "I'm into everything that I do. I don't do anything halfway." I told her. "That's probably why my ass is in here." I said.

"I think you're just misunderstood." She said.

"Me misunderstood, what about you?" I asked her.

We continued to pose, following the instructor, as we talked about our lives as misunderstood outcasts. S.J. went on to tell me about her husband. Her much older husband.

"I never met him before we were married." She told me. "It was not my decision to marry him." She said, quietly.

* * *

It was time for my therapy session. I walked, slowly, along the wall, making my way towards the door as the nurses continued to call my name.

"Miss Bampi, have a seat." Said the dark haired boy who couldn't have been any older than twenty six.

I rolled my eyes, withdrawing. *He couldn't possibly have enough life experience to understand my problems.* I thought to myself. I sat in the chair across from his and folded my arms. He began asking questions about my life and how I ended up in this hospital.

"How do you know when you're feeling good?" He asked.

"I don't know. You just Know." I replied.

"You can do better than that Rochelle." He said. "When you come across someone who you don't think is as smart as you, do you minimize your own intelligence? Or do you just become lazy?" He asked.

"Okay, I see what you're doing here." I told him. "All of those years of school are paying off." I said, jokingly. "I guess I know I feel good when I'm being productive, when I smile. and when I dance and sing around the house." I said. "I never really think about what makes me feel good. I'm usually too busy trying to survive."

"It looks to me that something has interrupted the girl who's simply trying to survive." He said. "Maybe you should be trying to do more than survive and this place, this world, will work more for you instead of against you."

I appreciated his words. We spoke for a little while longer. I was no longer suspicious of his motives.

We all met back in the day-room. My roommate, Bethany, and I all sat at the same table. We shared a box of colored pencils as we worked quietly on our butterfly pictures. This was a way to relieve stress and to meditate on how we could say the right things so we could get out of here. The room was quiet. You could hear the audience reactions coming from the television, you could hear nurses calling hospital codes over the speakers, and scattered chatter across the room was constant. Some patients talking in small groups and some talking to themselves. Everyone was in their own world. I passed a piece of paper to the S.J., who passed it to Bethany. Scribbled on it, were the words, *We are the sane ones and the staff are the crazy ones.* We all looked at one another, smiled, and continued our coloring projects.

Just as we began to bond, the chatter in the day-room began to subside. All eyes were directed toward the glass windows, separating us from the hallways and nurses station. I glanced up to find everyone staring at the latest arrival. We had already added crazy White boy Mike to the team. They let him out of his ropes and chains and allowed him to join the main crazy population. I couldn't believe that we were all mixed up together like that. Crazy White boy Mike would walk into the room, glowing, bright red. He'd bang his fists on the table and sit down. Everyone would move. Everyone but me.

Today our newest arrival was Jaquida. She was in college, at the local University. She had suffered a nervous breakdown on campus and they brought her here. She was a fluffy, Black girl. Her weave was matted and reaching up to the heavens. They brought her into the room where my fellow inmates were all watching her every move. She barely looked up from under the hair mangled across her face, as she snarled at the little Asian girl sitting near her. She looked over at me and I immediately broke eye contact. I was not about to be associated with her crazy ass. We were already the only two Black women in here. *One of us had to act like we had some sense.* I thought to myself.

It was time for our group session. S.J., Bethany, and I walked to the room together. We barely spoke. We took turns asking one another if each of us were alright and spent the remainder of the time in silence as we enjoyed each other's company.

"Today I want you to think about and define your triggers." The counselor was saying. "These are the things that may happen to cause an increase in your symptoms. Whatever they are. On this list, I want you to write them down." He instructed us. I began to write down the triggers I could think of.

Being judged.

Financial problems.

Family members.

As I begin to build my list I began to reflect, causing a clash between my conflicting emotions. I wanted to cry and yell, all at once. Without much clarity, I found myself longing for my old life, for the old Rochelle. Just as everyone begin finishing up. The sound of paper being torn to pieces filled the room. I looked over to where Jaquida was sitting and sure enough, baby girl was ripping up the assignment and any other piece of paper that she could get her hands on. She began to shout.

"You want to know my triggers? Your face is my triggers." She said.

I knew this wasn't about to go over well. I looked at S.J. and Bethany. I could tell that they were both afraid. I shot them a look that said, *Just chill out. We are going to see where this goes.* They both nodded slightly.

"I hate this place." She was screaming now and standing. "I want to go back to school. Give me my meds." She yelled.

All I could do was stare at her. I was waiting for the moment when her eyes would meet mine when the nurses sprung into action. The classroom door flung open and they poured into the room. Taking over the space. They rushed to Jaquida's side. Each of them making attempts to quiet her down so the class could continue.

"Jaquida," says one of the nurses, "Let's just sit down and breathe. You can't have any meds right now and you can't go home." She told her.

This was the last thing that baby girl wanted to hear. She began waving her arms around and pretending to swing on the staff. I don't know where that nurse pulled that needle from but she removed the cap and gave Jaquida a quick trip to lala land. They carried her to her room and we finished up our session.

I didn't see her again until later that night. It was after dinner and we were all waiting for our last phone calls of the night. Each of us patiently waiting our turns to use the phone. She was sitting near the corner. Draped in a blanket, she held her head down on the table. I grabbed a graham cracker and two juices and walked over to her table. I could see S.J. and Bethany's eyes follow me to the other side of the room. As I sat down, across from Jaquida, I could feel her feet shifting underneath the table.

"I'm Rochelle." I told her.

She didn't respond.

"I just wanted you to know that you're not alone." I continued. "Whatever it is that's bothering you, whatever you're going through, you need to fight it. That's your only way out of here. It's your only way back to reality." I said.

Lifting her head from the table, she said, "You don't know what I'm going through."

"You're right." I said. "But I bet you I've been through something similar or maybe even worse because it's not much that I haven't gone through. What matters is that we both are here, at this same point, right now. If no one else can understand you, I can." I told her. "You've got to try to pull it together. Stop giving them reasons to look at you. We are Black women. We do not have the luxury of clowning and showing our asses in here in front of all these white people." I finished.

"You right." She said.

"I know it. You just better not forget it and comb your hair. Make some phone calls, tell your people where you at , and try not to breakdown." I told her.

"Why are you so nice?" She asked.

"As opposed to what?" I replied.

It was time for my phone call home to Roan and I had no clue what I was going to say. I just needed to hear his voice and to make sure that my family wasn't brainwashing him, trying to turn him against me. I saw S.J. leave as I picked up the phone. I waved but she didn't notice my efforts.

It was great to hear Roan's voice and although he asked me over and over again, when I was coming home, I didn't worry as much about him hating me for putting him through this. He made me feel loved and forgiven with every word he uttered.

Just as we were saying, good night, an alarm went off and the doors began to lock, one after the other. The nurses began to run from behind the nurses station and we were all told to stay put. Someone ran by pushing a cart full of medical supplies and as my eyes followed them down the hall, I could see the staff going in and out of my room. Just as the alarm was silenced, it was S.J. I saw, being rolled down the hallway on a stretcher.

A Sisiter's Sister

It was only day three and I was already losing what mind I had left. From the crazy White boy Mike, to the Black girl meltdown, and down to my roommate's attempted suicide, I was drained. The medicine they had me taking, only made me feel worse. I was dragging my body around. I felt heavy and high as a kite. I didn't feel like myself. I was moving in slow motion.

I knew it was going to be a challenging day because today was visitation day. I knew my mom would be there. She told me on the phone, the night before, she'd be here to bring me some comfortable pajamas and socks. I told her to make sure that there were no drawstrings in the pants and to make sure she didn't bring anything liquid. The visit was uncomfortable. We barely spoke and I tried to make light of the situation but I couldn't. She kept telling me that I just needed to get my life together, and although this was true, I knew that there was so much more at stake here.

We went to exercise class after our family visits. I needed to blow off some steam and the instructor did not disappoint. I was punching and kicking the air with everything in me, trying to keep from crying. Our next group session forced us to think about how we feel when the things around us are breaking down or getting worse. I had to write down my own crisis indicators and the list was long. I no longer held any disdain toward therapy. I knew that my healing and decisions had consequences for not only myself, but for Roan as well.

We were all the same but different. By the end of the night we were all in the day room and you could tell that we were all tired. All of a sudden, crazy White boy Mike flies over Bethany's head and toward the skinny nerd. He punches him right in the jaw. His face turned beet red and as Mike removed his fist, you could see the imprints of his knuckles remaining, like a finger painting. We all moved to the side so the nurses could remove him from the room. We all went to bed afraid that night. I was more angry than I was afraid.

Day four and S.J. had returned to our room. I was very happy to see her but I didn't want to overwhelm her or make her feel bad, so I didn't say much.

"If you were doing well after that guy who's divorce you paid for, what really happened to land you in here?" She asked.

"After him, a few months after, I met Deidrick, online. It was during this time that I can say I actually met my own soul. I was just beginning to look at life totally different. I found it most difficult to have genuine relationships or friendships. I questioned everything. I never really knew when someone was being their honest to God genuine selves. I prepared myself for their judgment before they could get out their first word.

I longed for internal peace. I no longer wanted to give in to the desires of love and companionship. I wanted to be happy with who I was. I was seeing myself honestly for the first time in my life. life. Nature was beautiful and I wanted to enjoy it while it lasted, finally, awake. I wanted to be in touch with the land, my ancestors, my inner voice and still be seen as beautiful on the outside.

I wanted to be happy in my own skin. I wanted to be in love with my complexion, my hair texture and its length. I wanted my hairline to completely fill in. I wanted my son to be happy. I wanted him to grow up to be the best version of himself. I wanted to make him proud of me. I wanted to be vulnerable with someone. I wanted to be vulnerable with myself.

Around this time, I stopped wearing a wig when I left my house. This will seem like a small feet to some, but for me, this was the moment that was going to decide the rest of my life. Could I do this? Was I strong enough to admit that my weakness in not seeing my own beauty was most likely the cause of all that was wrong in my life?

To make matters worse, I wasn't even going out among strangers. I was going up the street, to my parents' house. Nevertheless, I wanted to look normal, beautiful. I wanted to feel pretty and to be seen as such. I wanted to hide my flaws and explode radiant sun kissed skin. I wanted to do this all while sporting my own hair and no makeup. Why? Because I wanted to be seen, I wanted them to finally see me and I didn't want to worry about if they approved of my appearance because for once, it was actually "My appearance".

I struggled with holding my head up high. I pulled into the driveway, turned the car off, sat there and tried to see if I was still breathing. I was afraid. Afraid that my younger sister would laugh or smirk during my visit and I would interpret her actions as that of negative judgment. God forbid she didn't like the way I looked and laughed at me.

"Looking back on it now, I can laugh. It's almost sickening that I cared what anyone thought about how I looked." I told S.J..

"I walked toward the house, veering off the black tar paved driveway, onto the concrete pathway toward the front door. My heart was beating loudly in my own ear. I fought the beads of moist forming at the tip of my hairline. As I walked, I'm thinking to myself, repeating in my head the mantra I made up in the car on my way there, *you are beautiful, you are pretty, be beautiful, be pretty, believe it and everyone else will too.*

I reached the porch steps where my son and nephew appeared running from the side of the house chasing bubbles and with my father sitting on the step. I could tell they were wondering what was going on with my head but I said my hellos and continued inside.I felt as if people, my family members, were not pleased with my appearance or that I looked ugly.

I wanted to die right there. No one said a word. I wanted to cry but how could I explain to them that I was crying because I didn't like the way that I looked and I feared they didn't either and that this made me afraid and sad? Why did I care so much? Why couldn't I just be happy with myself. Happy with who I am?

I was never satisfied. It was always I can change this, make this bigger, this smaller, grow this, cut this, shave those, straighten that. It was so uncomfortable sitting there. I tried to catch a glance of either my mom or sister staring at me or smirking. I was driving myself crazy. I had to get the hell out of there. I made up an excuse to leave. With child in tow, I marched to the car, panting, damn near about to pee on myself. *Got to get in the car and back the car out of the driveway,* I'm thinking to myself. *Got to drive and not look back.* I turn the corner and I can almost breathe again.

I had just had a full blown anxiety attack and all because I think I'm ugly. It was like my mind was fighting my brain. Stay with me. It was as if my mind didn't think I was beautiful or attractive. My mind believed that others find me unattractive as well. My brain didn't care because it's not like we can change our appearance or make everyone on this forsaken planet happy, so get over it.

I looked in the mirror a lot after that. I would just stand there, doing nothing, staring at myself. I looked at ever hair follicle, every hair shaft and pore. I examined my eyebrows, feeling the texture of each strand following the natural arch. This was my therapy. My daily love on me time. I began to treat my hair with vitamins, herbs, and oils. I worked on the mixture for almost a year before I perfected the formula.

As my hair began to grow, I saw parts of my soul beginning to reappear. I really hadn't seen myself without weave or with my own natural full head of hair in over 20 years. I didn't know what I should expect to see at the end of this journey because I didn't really know what I looked like. Maybe that's why I don't like what I see when I see myself. Because I know that until my hairline is full and my thin edges fill in, I will never really see myself as I should be seen." I told her.

"Vulnerability with one's self is never meant to feel comfortable. You must step out of your comfort zone. At least that's what I tell myself. You have to change your normal behaviors if you truly want something different in life. You can't continue to do the same thing over and over again because it's obviously not working. If I really want to be happy with myself 99.8% of the time then I need to learn to love myself. How can I ask anyone else to love me if I don't love me?

When people tell me they think I'm attractive, pretty, or beautiful, I usually will smile an awkward embarrassed smile and say thank you but inside, inside I'm questioning their motives. I'm telling myself that, *if they really knew me and how I really looked, they wouldn't think I looked so nice. I'm fake.* I feel like when you take away the weave, the foundation, the lip liner, the concealer, the mascara, the eye liner, the brow pencil, the lip stick, the contour then what am I? What am I but me and me isn't enough? Isn't good enough.

I can't tell anyone how I really feel about myself. When I walk outside I become guarded but I pretend to be open, confident and friendly. That's why I started my own hair care line for women just like me." I finished.

"So you just started a hair care line?" S.J. asked.

"Yeah, something like that. But I barely had any support. I was back at my parents house, well into my thirties, with Roan, talking about making a hair growth formula from my own research and marketing it online. My parents laughed at me and told me to get a real job. I called some of my friends and reached out to some of my social media contacts. I was able to sell out in my first month of starting Journey Natural Hair Growth Products. I loved it but I couldn't sustain the business alone. With my parents constantly nagging at me to get a real job, go on interviews, clean up their house, and watch my kid at all times, I hardly had the energy to fulfill orders, post online or answer customer questions.

I was missing orders and the bills were adding up. With no real startup money and little to no guidance, I began to crash. During this time, I gave into my parents request and took that ever so debilitating position at the post office. I worked my ass off. I put up with ghetto girls who'd fight you if they thought you looked at their man. I dealt with coworkers having attitudes because they thought I was trying to make them look bad by the way I put my all into my work. These people were crazy for real. There are several straws that broke this camel's back. I didn't just give up." I told her.

"During this time I was lonely, stressed, and making the dumbest decision of my life, to form a relationship with my little sister. My father had been saying something about me being a better big sister and she had her own place now so I wanted to hang out with her in her environment and on her terms.

Kelly was rough around the edges and a big girl. She preferred to hang out with the hood side of the family and was always trying to show you, how down she really was. She dated dope boys and although she didn't go off to New York in her teens, she found her share of drama. She would accuse me of thinking too much of myself and thinking I was better than her. This couldn't have been further from the truth but her mind was made up.

While my business was failing, I tried to entertain myself by staying out late and drinking. I was smoking like crazy and trying to feel something. Anything. I was having sex with random guys, I met through her. It was a regular hoe fest over there. Kelly had a boyfriend who would stop over from time to time. He wasn't much to look at, by my standards, tall, dark, skinny, and missing teeth with his pants sagging. I was not impressed. He'd get drunk and pass out on the couch often.

One night, I stayed over. I was drunk so Kelly and her friend put me in her bed. When I woke, Kelly was gone to work, both of our kids stayed home from school, and her man was still there. Since she was at work, I figured I'd cook breakfast for the boys, clean up our mess, and make the house look nice for her when she came home. Before I could finish my project, she was home. I asked if everything was okay. I could tell she had an attitude. Roan and I left. A few weeks later while she and her man were arguing, he told her, "That's why I fucked your sister."

I don't know why he said that because it never happened. My guess was that she questioned him about the day I left and he, while drunk, used her insecurities against her. Whatever the reason, when this got back to me, I was pissed. She told everyone. Our parents, distant cousins, and mutual friends. The worst part was that she actually believed him. I think she wanted to believe him. I hated her.Afterwards, my parents blamed me. They said that I should've known better to try and hang around with people her age.

I was more than unhappy. I was having no luck with dating, add on top of that stress, my business crashing, and my unfortunate employment and I was ready to explode. That's when I decided to move out and into Diedrick's.

By March, I was back and although I was mentoring and trying to hide what I was going through, I still ended up here, having this nervous breakdown. " I said.

"Yes you did." Replied S.J..

We made our way to the class room for our day five therapy session. On today's schedule was our WRAP Program. This was our wellness recovery action plan and we had to each complete one before we could be released. I filled in as many lines as possible but some of the questions I couldn't take seriously. No one compartmentalizes their lives like this. After I completed my action plan, it was time for me to make my phone call to my parents on speaker, to see if they would agree to let me return home.

The notion was overly embarrassing. I was sitting in the office with two staff members next to me listening in as my mother made requests that I keep the house clean, get a job, and follow their rules if I want to return to their house. I agreed. As we walked out of the office, the counselor turned to me and said, "I'm sorry that you have to go back to that."

I was grateful for his sympathy.

My last two days in the mental ward we unusually calm. I gave Jaquida my number and promised to call her when we made it to the outside. The social worker paid me a visit and left me more confused than I already was, and S.J. and I had to say our goodbyes. I didn't want to leave her. Even after all I've been through with humans, she still felt like a sister's type of sister and I desperately wanted to be there for her. The wounds on her wrist were still fresh. I looked at her sad eyes as I held her hand and spoke.

"You are worth living." I told her. "And you're worth living a good life, in this life, right now. Take what's yours." I said. We hugged and waved as I walked through the doors of the mental ward. I passed the security guards and walked toward the revolving doors. I didn't know what was waiting on the other side but I did know that I would have to find out.

* * *

Realistic Tears

I've cried so many tears that my hands will always drip cold sweat upon my own heart.

Faced with false realities, I've been staring at the same pile of dirty laundry for over a week now.

Space and time nonexistent.

Thoughts of a fantastical life with you remains persistent. Too many opportunities were provided. I'll excuse you once and more. Your heart and mind are divided.

Pacify me as you would an infant. Expectations prepared for you to be inconsistent.

Do we converse in a tongue we mutually understand? I sit here, at the edge, of the bed.

Hands wet from the sweat escaping the eyes in my face. Lies feel better. Lie to me.

Tell me only the words I need you to see me hear. Smother me with fictitious I love You's.

Hold my head to your soul and put your lying hands in my natural hair.

Kiss my lips with closed eyes. Make love to my body until it cries.

Sex and money are your Gods.

Sadness becomes my high.

Anger my stimulant.

Pain my motivation.

Tears my awakening.

My worse fear is your inevitable impact on my entire being.

You promise to fall off the earth the ways my tears are guaranteed to fall from the eyes in my face.

Maybe if I cry, you'll stay.

JouRney Girls

The car ride home was silent. I was high off of the medicine still. Lost. Dazed overwhelmed. I realize, as my mother drove us away from the hospital and towards the house, that I had stopped living my life when it all got bad and went to hell. I couldn't catch up on the bills, their expectations, who I was portraying myself as. I couldn't catch a hold of my own life. I didn't feel relieved as I looked out of the window, trying to locate an area of familiarity. I felt more lost now then when I was inside.

The moment I stepped foot back into the house, I felt the pressure. When I took the medicine I looked and was high. My father would walk by and make little comments. I wanted to work on my hair care line but everyone pushed me to get a job. I took a job at a gas station up the street from the house. It wasn't much but it was enough to shut my folks up for a short period of time.

I started to date one of the guys that I met earlier, through Kelly. He was an alcoholic battling his own depression. This was the worst time for me to try and date anyone. I had no freedom. I had to sneak him in my house and anytime I wanted to be alone without a kid, I had to pay money, I didn't have, for a room. It was exhausting. His alcoholism became mine.

Taking control of my thoughts again, I switch my attention back over to "Roan". He's partially to blame for my body hurting each morning and why I have to perform a Yoga- ish , meditation- ish type of stretch each time I wake up. If he sleeps in my bed, my entire body hurts the next day. I try to make deals with him to make him sleep in his own room, across the hall. Even after promising him extra computer or video game time, he always ends up in my bed.

I looked over at my son taking up more than half of this twin size bed. "Roan", I playfully and in a sing song voice, whispered into his ear as I leaned in for a kiss to wake him. "Roan" I repeated. "King Roan wake up sleepy head." Forcefully rocking his slim frame, I uncurl his gigantic legs. "Wake up or I'm going to tickle you." I said loudly. He didn't budge. Typical. "What six-year-old sneaks and stays awake all night watching videos then wants to sleep all day?" I asked him. "Fine, I'm going to play my wake-up song that I want to hear and I don't care if you like it or not".

I could see his eyes begin to twitch. His long black eyelashes danced as he began to open his eyes for the first time. I tried not to show how ecstatic I was. Started to wait to see if he was happy that I woke him or if he was angry. He's usually happy. "Hi Baby" I said.

"Hi Mommy," he replied. Every time he called me mom, it gave me butterflies and made me want to cry. Just a few years ago I couldn't get him to call me mommy to save my life! He is the sound my heart makes when it's the quietest. He's as compassionate as I'd hope to be one day.

In the bedroom of my parent's home, Roan, my first son and only child, lay with his feet pressed into the back of what felt like, my entire body. For someone so young, his legs were long and skinny. His bones felt like knives being forced into my back while I slept. I loathed being here. Not because the house was unlivable or because we were treated unfairly. I hated living here because living here meant that I needed them and they knew it. I had only recently returned to live with my parents but I was counting down the days when we could leave.

"Is it time for our wake-up song?" He asked with a kind of old man I don't want to be bothered so I'll only open one eye, look on his face. I couldn't help but to look at him and smile. He couldn't help but smile back. We were kindred spirits that way, he and I. He was my son but he was so much more than that. He offered a window for me to see love, genuine love and he gave me a mirror in which I was able to see my soul.

"Oh, you think it's funny." I said while trying to get under the covers to tickle him. "It's not funny, and I will beat you up and take a bite out of your toe toes if you keep laughing at mama." I warned him.

"Okay okay." He insisted, trying to interrupt the bite I had planned for his little tiny toes with the palm of his hand. "Don't eat me, I'm not edible, he proclaimed."

Caught off guard by his verbiage, I went in for a kiss instead of the pending bite. "I love you pumpkin." I told him.

"I love you too mom, you're the best mom in the whole wide world." He replied.

It was because of my love for him that we ended up back in this house, where I never had any visitors, had to hide my true self more often than not, where every move my son made was questioned or ridiculed. The person I had to pretend to be while we lived here was slowly killing me. I knew it, Roan didn't. I'd be forced to tell him the truth if we ever had to make a run for it in the dark of night. That was our relationship. He was older than five years old but intelligent so I tried to be upfront with him about life and my mistakes.

"Mom is far from perfect." I would tell him. "I make mistakes just as you do. The difference is mommy's mistakes affect more people and on a greater scale so I have to try not to mess up as often."

I picked up my phone to play the wake-up song. I knew what song he wanted because we did this same routine every day. I made this a part of our daily schedule due to him getting in trouble in school and not wanting him to have so many rough mornings. So we started singing and dancing every morning before school. I hated having to get up so early and being happy. I did it for him and only him. We got pretty good and our dance routine was jazzy too.

I held my breath for a moment while I searched for the song in my playlist. I knew once I pushed the play button it was game on and he wouldn't stop dancing once he heard the music. He sat straight up once the chipmunks began to sing the kids version of a popular hip hop song. I knew it was game on as he hopped out of the bed and started doing the running man. I followed him out of the bedroom, music blasting from the speakers of my smartphone. We did our two step all the way to the bathroom door. Inside, we were singing and dancing, brushing our teeth and getting powered up for his day of school in a place where very few people looked like him. I was preparing him for life in these moments and it seemed all but necessary.

Kenny G's Summertime blasting from those same speakers. It's my turn now. "Bye Rody ." I waved goodbye as he ran naked to the bedroom with his clothes in hand.

"I'm going to get dressed mom." he yelled. I replied to him with mutual enthusiasm, "Okay Rody." Like clockwork he's out of my eyesight and for the first time this morning, I can concentrate on me. My movements turned into deep meditation as I sway back and forth eyes almost closed hands clasped together like lovers do when they dance. I'm truly at peace here with the doors closed, water running, music playing, just the mirror and me. I've been going through something lately. My mind feels cloudy then I lose myself, inside myself, moments at a time.

I was in the shower when I heard the door open before I could grab my bath towel. Stepping onto the wet, fluffy, grey area rug that sits outside of the bathtub, I reached for a towel to cover myself. I quickly reached for the door knob. The steam from the shower had fogged the entire mirror and the steam tried to escape once the door crept open. I stuck my head out.

"What's going on?" I asked waiting for anyone to respond. I knew who would respond. Just like I knew exactly what she was going to say. She rarely says anything positive so I know as soon as she opens her mouth, I'm going to want her to close it.

"What's all that noise?" I heard my mother say. "It's just Rody." I explained. I tried to give her a moment to be a nonjudgmental parent but her facial expression said it all. Reading minds, isn't one of my super powers, but I can always tell when Karen, my mother, wasn't pleased.

She carried herself like a carefree Black woman. She pretended to be innocent but I knew better. Most of my wars have been fought with her as the opposing country. We never saw eye to eye and I can't recall a time when we've liked each other. She was controlling, manipulative, and gossiped about everyone. She saw wrong in everything and everyone but herself.

Standing there in my towel, I ask her. "Is there something wrong?"

"You should teach your son to be quieter." She fired back.

That shit went all the way through my body. I was already walking around the house on eggshells. Every time Rody made a noise, I had to run and tell him to be quiet because the last thing I wanted was for her to come out and say something to me. I'd lose it. I'd blow up and go off, then there would be no coming back from that. I knew that she had no idea of her imminent screaming match so I decided to retreat into the bathroom to calm myself down.

Quietly I closed the door, as to not make her think I intended to show my anger by slamming "her" bathroom door in "her" house. Internally, I wanted to slam that door hard as hell so she'd know I gave not one care about her knowing if I'm angry or not. As the door closed I caught a glance of myself in the mirror. I didn't like to look at myself anymore and It's been a very long time since the last time I liked what I saw in it anyway. I closed my eyes, put my head back and rolled my neck around until I heard several cracks, each more satisfying than the other. I ran the water in the sink to help me focus.

My mind continued to replay the last scene from beginning to end, hoping to find an error in my assumption. I tried to make myself see the good in my mother. I knew she really didn't mean any harm. She didn't know how much her behavior towards me, affected me so much.

I rebelled against her from the start. Karen was an always right, her way or the highway type of person. You can't have a kid like me and think you're always right. I will argue the breaks off of you. I never said I was right but I damn sure had a theory. Karen, my mother, wasn't like this. She believed what she believed. If she questioned anything she learned, I never knew it. Her traditional Black home background would not allow for her to imagine outside of her greatly migrated, societal norms. So much so, there have been occasions when my mom asked, "why do you use words that I don't understand, why do you have to use big words?" To which I'd reply, "what's a big word?" yeah I was a complete jerk.

Lately, everything that I've ever had to deal with has become a weight on my shoulders. My body feels heavy and it's becoming more and more difficult to pretend to smile. I had to make a decision and I had to make it now. I put on my clothes, put some papers in a bag, sent Rody off to the school bus and returned to the house to perform the final task on my list.

Standing in the doorway of the bedroom she shared with my father, Karen, my mother, never making eye contact, nervously moves random items from one side of her dresser to the other. "What Chelle?" she said disdainfully. I hand her the two-pocket folder and wait for her to say something. My eyes half closed. My adrenaline is pumping and I can feel the sweat beads falling from my fingertips onto the carpeted floor.

"Do you know what that was I just handed you?" I asked.

"I think." She answered with her nose scrunched up and her eyes rolling to the side of her head. I had handed her a folder that contained the records of my life. My social security information, Roan's birth certificate and insurance info, and medical information for us both. Giving her this folder right after I had a huge altercation with one of my parents should be enough to warn her that I'm not okay right now and I'm really close to jumping over the edge. You'd think she'd respond with a little more compassion, sensitivity, damn just act like a caring mother.

"Is that it Chelle?" She asked? My mother always has a damn attitude. I wish she'd call me by my name. No one calls me by my real name and I'm just over it. I'm about to start wearing a name tag with the phonics breakdown in parentheses.

"Yes, that's it. I just wanted you to have our information in case anything happened to me. So that's all of our info right there and any important phone number." I explained to her. I exited just as awkwardly as I entered the doorway to her room. I wondered if she remembered that I was just in a crazy house not too long ago.

I returned to my room about 20 steps away from Karen's door and sat on the edge of my twin size bed. I have no clue how I'm supposed to feel. I'm mad but I'm mad at how she acts toward me. I know better than to go and give her anything but I did that dumb shit anyway. I don't even know why I let her get under my skin.

"Cheeeeeellllllllle", I hear my father, Roy yell. *"Damn"*, I think to myself. "*why can't I have one moment to myself?*" I'm pissed in here. I'm screaming into pillows and silently screaming while stretching because for some reason, this feels good.

"Yeeeesssssss", I reply like a church choir responds in the cover of Shekinah Glory's "My Heart Says Yes." I'm up to my feet now. Body feeling stiff and hurting because for some reason every time I sit down and get up I hurt, but I stand up anyway and begin walking towards my bedroom door towards the voice of my father. I vocally respond for a second time just to let him know that I heard him and I'm on my way. . I walk downstairs to see what the hell Roy could possibly want. I just left another traumatic and dramatic situation. Can you let me adjust?

I didn't want to come back here. I'm in my thirties and the last thing I wanted to do was go back and live with my parents. I've made so many mistakes that this entire situation was inevitable and unavoidable. I should have seen this coming. My therapist likes to remind that I can't predict the future so I should refrain from being upset with myself when things happen that I felt I could have prepared for.

As I reached the bottom of the staircase, I hear my father say, "we've given her all this and she walks around here with an attitude and acts like she can't get out of bed." I almost fell to the floor right then and there. What have you given me, I wanted to scream? Did you teach me how to function in this world, did you show me how to use an education to my advantage, did you show me how to get a 6 figure job or was that me? Did you give me anything to believe in besides you going to work every day and hoping that your children one day become good people? What have you given me?

Every time I run into the arms of an undeserving man, to a foreign city, to a high paying job in places you've never heard of, every time I hit a downward spiral, you are at the center of it. You want so much from me when there is only so little that I have left to give and that is reserved for my son.

After leaving my last relationship I would have rather gone to a shelter than to return here but you made me return. You threatened to take away my child if I did not. Now I have nothing. Now I am nothing. I am more of nothing now than I was before. I have no job. My passions you see as hobbies. You want me to be just like you but I'm not you, I'm not any of you.

I wanted to shout this to scream it loudly for all to hear but instead I grabbed my bag and walked out. I got into my little four door sedan and began to drive. I knew that in order to live, I would have to die. I packed in my car, the little girl with the school uniform and braids with beads, the girl with no rhythm, the lover not a fighter, the lost one, the runner, the insecure, ashamed, embarrassed, the fearful, the naive, the bald headed one, the one who doesn't know who she is or where she came from, the one who lost her strength and never had a true identity, the depressed one, the one that allows anxiety to control her, the one that allows the stigma of mental health in the black community from keeping her from getting help. I loaded them all into the car, wrote a letter, then drove into oncoming traffic.

I was forced onto the median before I could hit any vehicles. I placed the car in park and got out. My legs gave out as soon as I was standing. I fell to the ground and burst into tears. I knew I had to go back. I couldn't possibly leave Roan with those people. I was going to wait for him to return and then we would leave for good this time.

The stress from losing my job at the gas station and not being able to sustain my company, and failing my son was too much to bare. My body became sick. Alcohol was all I took in until Roan arrived. By this time, I was good and drunk. I needed someone to take care of me and I knew that I couldn't ask my mother. I asked her if the guy I was dating could come over. Her answer was a simple, "no."

I explained that I didn't feel well and I just needed someone to care for Roan while I recovered. She smirked and laughed and told me to get out of her face. I turned to leave, calling her a controlling bitch on my way out of the door. She jumped from where she had been lying, playing games, in bed, on her phone, and stood on the other side of her bedroom threshold. She laughed and said, "you better go take your medicine, crazy.

"You're the one that needs therapy." I shouted back.

As I made my way to my bedroom we continued our shouting match. Roan was screaming and asking that we both please be quiet. She pulled out her phone and began to record. She asked that I return the phone she had given me and she began to read all of the messages the man I was dating and I had exchanged and send them to my sister.

This was the last straw. I began to pack Roan's things and put them into the car. I didn't have anywhere to go and it was nighttime now but I knew that drastic measures were necessary. I slept in the car in the driveway, until the next day.

I saw my mom leave the next day. She backed out of the driveway as I started to open my eyes. With her out of the way I could initiate my plan and get the hell out of here. I ran in the house trying to grab as much as I could. My father was walking around in his rob making comments under his breath as I went from room to room packing things. I knew that I needed to grab Roan and get to a shelter.

As Roan and I made our way to the car, Kelly pulls up and blocks my car in. She began yelling and cursing, calling me stupid for leaving and going to a shelter. She said I was crazy and retarded for cursing out our mom, the night before. I didn't care what she said. I took my time putting my seat-belt on and buckling in Roan. As I put the car in reverse, the passenger door swung open and Kelly came flying over. She was grabbing my hair, pulling at my clothes and punching me in the face. My foot was on the break but the car was still in gear. I was cursing at her and yelling for her to let me go. I yelled for Roan to get out of the car as I put it in park.

I jumped out the car and glided across the hood. Once I got to her, I could see her son screaming and yelling while my father held her baby boy. We were in the middle of the driveway. It was a full on brawl. From time to time, my father would kick me to try to keep me down on the ground. There was no way that I was going to stay down. We fought all the way back inside the house. We went up and down the stairs. They tried to take Roan. I would free him and then fight them off again until Roan and I made it to the backyard. As Kelly pounded on my back with her fists, I hovered over Roan, protecting him like a shield as he cowered beneath me.

My father called the police. When they arrived, it was Officer Schwartz again.

"I think it's time for you to go your own way Rochelle." He told me. "Don't let trying to be who they need you to be, kill you." He said. Roan and I rode in the ambulance to the hospital together as I decided to press charges against my family or not.

Who can I call? I thought to myself. Shelters were an option but I really didn't want to have to do that to Roan. I started to look through my purse, looking for any cash, cards, a miracle. Roan was being entertained by the nurses as I finished up my police report. At the bottom of my bag, there was something that caught my eye. Something I had never seen before. I hadn't used the bag that much because it reminded me of my crazy house stay but I was running away again so I grabbed it.

Investigation of the card found the letters "IHG" on the front and a bar-code on the back. It wasn't a bar-code. It was one of those codes that you use with your phone. A QVR code. I scanned the code on the card with my phone. Immediately, a notification appeared on the phone.

"Home girl help." Could you use a true home girl? Select option 1. I selected the first option. The next screen told me, D*on't move a home girl is on the way!*

I continued my conversation with the doctor and nurses. Just as I begin to prepare to be discharged, a familiar face popped her head around the corner and into the room.

"Going somewhere? Need a ride?" She asked. It was Claudia. The nurse from the emergency room where I had my crisis intake.

"I see you found my card." She said pointing to my phone. "Let's get out of here. Let's go Roan." She said as we grabbed our things and followed her to the exit.

"I can't believe you're here." I said.

"Believe it homegirl." She replied.

I began to worry about my car and belongings. She set me straight about worrying about the wrong things. I wanted to lash out but she was right. I had bigger things to worry about.

"Are you hungry?" Asked Claudia.

I wasn't hungry but Roan was. We stopped to grab him something quick before Claudia said, "Tonight it's late so we will stay at my place."

"I don't want to accept the help." I told her.

"You already have." She said. "You did the moment you loaded that app onto your phone." She continued. "You need to let this happen. Girl we gone get you together." She exclaimed.

We all settled into her apartment. Roan was overjoyed to learn that Claudia had a dog a Yorkie shih tzu mix. Sugar. I apologized to roan for everything that went on. For everything that he saw. I promised him that I would always protect him. Then I cried my eyes out in the bathroom. I could hear Claudia on the phone. She set up a meeting. For tomorrow, early. I heard her clearly confirm the date and time. She said, "All home girls on deck." As she hung up the phone.

It was already late so I put roan to bed. Claudia had put out a fresh pair of pajamas on the bed for me. I appreciated the extra mile she was going to make us feel welcomed. My head was still spinning. She offered me a glass of wine, told me to help myself to food in the kitchen, and made sure I knew what movie channels she had. There wasn't any unnecessary talking. It wasn't long before we were both dozing off.

"Claudia I have failed and I don't think I can get back up this time." I told her.

"No girl, you only fail when you stop trying. Are you still trying? Okay then. Life is a journey and we are on it right now girl. Good night." She finished as we both made our way to our rooms for the night.

"Good night, Claudia." I said. "Thank you, again." I told her.

II

Fetal Position

A place of comfort
A place where I reluctantly go to die.
A place where I meet myself for engaging discussions,
regarding my many mistakes.
Pillow in arms cradled like the husband I'll never have, so I don't
feel alone with myself.

Rescue Mission

It was early, that next morning, when the sounds of an up-tempo Caribbean song began to bleed through the cracks between the doors.

"Hey Home-girl." I heard Claudia answer the phone as she slowly and quietly closed her bedroom door.

"Roan." I called out while pulling back the blankets that were draped across him to cover his body and head. "Baby it's time to wake up." I whispered into his ear as I kissed the sides of his face. I wrapped his feet into mine and covered our bodies fully underneath the covers.

"What?" Roan gushed displaying his elevated cheekbones.

"What?" I repeated as if puzzled by his disrespectful greeting.

"I mean huh, Ma'am." he replied.

"Yeah okay," I said. "You better watch all of that." I said with a bit of sass. We both laughed as I poked at his thin body. "Okay." I said. "Who are we?" I asked.

"Bampis." He replied.

"And what are we?" I asked.

"Strong." He said in a way that made me believe he finally was on board with what I had known all along.

"And what do we do?" I asked him.

His jolt from underneath the blankets shook the entire bed as he leaped to his feet shouting, "We keep it moving." He kicked his leg out and did his best MJ impersonation. Lost in laughter, I didn't see Claudia standing with her cocoa smooth face contrasting against the vanilla bedroom walls, at the door.

"Oh my God." I said. "I'm so sorry that we are so loud this morning."

"Yeah." Yelled Roan, " We're Bampi's." He belted out with a sound that seemed prehistoric at its origin.

" Boy did you just growl? " I asked him.

"I'm so sorry." I told Claudia. with her plump lips on full display, in her fire alarm red lipstick, it was clear that she was ready to go.

"I'm so glad you all are awake because I'm going to need you to get ready so we can head out ASAP. I want you to keep that same energy." She smirked and winked at Roan.

"I guess it's time to snap back to reality." I uttered to myself. Claudia's look revealing her sensitive ears, I rolled my eyes, fell back on the bed and smothered my face with the pillow, I used only a few moments ago to wake Roan up.

"What is going on?" I asked. "There's a lot of phones ringing, not that I'm listening or anything, but I haven't heard a black woman refer to another black woman as a home girl so many times since like 96." I said quizzically slowly peeking out from under the blanket. Sitting upright, I reminded Claudia that I needed to deal with what had just landed us in the hospital only yesterday. " I need to go handle that situation and figure out what to do next with my life." I told her.

"You know what?" She said. "I'm glad you said that. Hold that thought. I'm going to take Roan and get him started with breaking his fast and you take your time and get ready. Meet us in the kitchen when you're done." She instructed me.

"Roan, remind your mommy of who she is one more time for me please." She said as she locked her fingers with his pulling him towards the door where she had been standing this entire conversation.

Roan, leaping from the bed, still grasped by her clasped fingers, landed next to her on the shaggy rug, guarding the bedroom door.

"What is your mommy?" I heard Claudia chant as she led Roan to the kitchen.

"A Bampi." I heard Roan reply.

Dressed in the threads that were laid across the bed once I returned from a hot shower, I made my way to the kitchen dreading the conversation that seemed unavoidable.

"Have several seats child." She said, gesturing to the tall bar stools across from the counter from where she was leaning, scrolling down her phone. I took the center bar-stool as she placed her phone face down on the counter-top.

"Why were you smiling so hard at your phone when I walked in? Where is Roan? Seriously what's going on here?" I asked her.

"Well, I'm smiling and laughing at my phone, nosy, because my home girls are funny and they don't have any sense which is why I love them. Roan is getting dressed, I had one of my girls drop off a few outfits for him while you were in the shower. I hope you don't mind and to be honest I really don't care if you do, and finally, this," she gestured in a circular motion, "this is an IHG Rescue Mission." She finished.

I was hearing all that she had to say and my attempts to take it all in were failing miserably. I lowered my head into my hand and allowed my elbows to rest standing at the counter that served as the island. Looking directly into her big beautiful brown eyes I said, "Well, you told me a lot but I still don't know nothing." We both burst into a tearful laughter. "But I do want to tell you that I appreciate the outfits that you gave Roan, so there's that." I said as the sound of our laughter began to echo throughout the kitchen and into the hallway.

"Seriously, Claudia." I said trying to return to the subject of what she had just referred to as an IHG Rescue Mission. "Claudia what the hell is that?" I asked. "Is this serious? Why can't you just come out and tell me?" I asked.

"I've been telling you. You just aren't listening." She yelled.

"Well okay then,". I said. "You got one more again to yell at me little sister." I told her.

"That's true," she said. "I am the little sister but I'm exactly what you need right now, we all are." She finished. "Me and my homegirls that you keep eavesdropping on." she giggled. " Honestly the secrecy is necessary. We don't know if you're ready to accept what it is that we're offering." She exclaimed. " We can't just be telling you all of our business until we know that you will be discreet about membership into our organization and what it is that we actually do." She finished.

"Ahhh it IS a cult ." I announced. " You're trying to get me to join a cult." I was messing with her and she knew it. I had come this far blindly, I was willing to keep going.

"You do know that you have issues right?" she divulged as she checked the time on her phone. "You should break your fast too." she said, pointing towards Roan who was finally dressed.

"Well look who decided to join us." I said, motioning for Roan to stand near me. " Did you brush your teeth? Did you wash your face? Did you put lotion on your face?" I asked him. with a quick nod, yes, he was off again Searching for Sugar the shih tzu.

"This is what I can tell you Rochelle," Claudia explained.

"I'm a member of an organization called International Homegirls. We are a group of all types of women around the world, that believe in reaching our best potential, living our best lives, while helping other women do the same. We are committed to the betterment of each other but first to ourselves. Sometimes, we come across women who are just like us except they have dealt with trauma, hardships, or some obstacle that held them back. Sometimes we come across these women and when we see that they may need us, we wait until no one is watching and we slip a home girl RM card into their purse. We watched you at the hospital, we followed your business attempts and your parenting on social media. We read between the lines of statuses so fake it made no sense. We did that and we saw in you a woman worth saving. Now we just have to figure out if you know that she's worth saving." She said genuinely. "These are women whom I trust with my life, your life, and even Roan's life. We just want to give you a little help." She finished. I knew that she was waiting for me to say something.

"Why me and how does all of this work?" I asked." I can't afford to pay anything. We need a place to stay and I need to wrap my head around all of this." I replied.

"Why not you Rochelle?" She asked Compassionately. "Don't you think you deserve to be rescued?" She stood back from the counter and looked around the room. "I don't see anyone else running to save you and how long have you been trying to save yourself, alone?" Another question we both knew needed no verbal response. " You have to look at it like this Chelle, you're in your thirties, you have a son that you are raising alone, you've been through more than a little bit and depending on your definition of success, you haven't been successful in years. You could really use the support. So can we go now? Are you ready?"

She was right, I thought to myself I do need support if I'm going to get through this with my mental health intact.

"Yes, I'm ready." I told her.

The sun was already scorching down on us as we made our way from Claudia's building to the front doors of the double decker, blacked out trailer bus, parked directly in front of the entrance. There were no big graphics posted on either side of the bus. Just a simple decal on the front window with the letters IHG. The doors opened and Claudia pushed pass us and began to make her way up the steps.

"Hey homegirls." she greeted everyone as she motioned for Ro and I to climb aboard. "This is Santina B. She's responsible for all of the swag and IHG gear you saw at my place and even the shirt you're wearing now."

I waved at Santina as she rose from the driver's seat and motioned for an embrace saying, "I give hugs, hey girl hey, hey little man." She said while kneeling to shake Ro's hand. I noticed that underneath her boy cut suit jacket and bow-tie, she was wearing the same shirt that I was wearing but it was in a different color. Hers was purple. In fact, we all were wearing the same shirt. Only one woman wore the exact pink one that I was told to put on earlier this morning.

"This is Patricia, she's also going through intake." Claudia pointed to the woman dressed like me.

"Nice to meet you." I said.

"Hey what up?" She said loudly. She must have seen the surprise in my face after her greeting because she changed her tone and repeated my original greeting in a cadence similar to my own. "Nice to meet you." She said.

"And this is Kenya." Claudia said while hugging the woman sitting across from Patricia. "This is our residential communications and social media badass. You'll get to know her very well." She said. "This is Kenya's daughter, we call her Bug." Just as she called her name, a skinny brown skin girl with curly hair came from behind her back. "Bug this is Roan, Roan this is Bug." She introduced them to one another.

"Do you want to go play with my slime?" Bug asked Ro.

"Yea, can I mom?" Ro asked.

"Sure can." I replied.

"It's okay ma'am," Kenya said in an accent that screamed Mississippi bread. "There is a play area in this little homegirl mobile. Bug knows all of the best hiding places. Don't worry they'll be okay." She assured me.

"Thank you." I told her.

"Everybody's going to be okay because I'm the one driving this bad boy." I heard Santina utter as she made her way back into the driver's seat. "Now I know that it looks like an office in here but I don't want y'all to get carried away walking around here like we ain't on fifty-leven Wheels." she yelled out. "Whose playlist are we listening to?" She surveyed the crowd gathering around Kenya's desk area, where she was still conducting intake with Patricia. I could tell that Patricia was just as anxious as I was by the way she continued raking her hands through her naturally straight blonde hair. I knew what it felt like to be the only black girl in a crowded room so I could only imagine what she was going through. Breaking the silence to answer Santina's question, Claudia yelled to the front of the bus.

"Whatever you do, don't play Nadia's playlist. She listens to ancient music." Everyone laughed. I thought to myself, *Hey I like ancient music,* I just might like this Nadia girl.

"Okay Claudia, don't make me change that purple shirt to a pink one." The Voice came from the lower level of the bus. She was coming up the stairs. She was sporting short black hair and a pair of glasses that screamed I teach somebody's kids. She grabbed both of my hands and stood back, looking me over.

"Yeah you're still in there." she said. "We're just going to have to nudge you back out and into civilization." She finished.

"This Magnificent woman is Nadia." Claudia said. "She's one of our main coaches and she develops and approves all of our educational material. I know all of this sounds like a lot but trust me it's not, you'll catch on." she winked.

"If Nobody wants to tell me what music to play, I'm playing what I like." Santina yelled.

"Has she met Julie yet?" Nadia asked.

"No, I haven't gotten that far in the tour yet." Claudia replied.

"Oh okay, well I will see you when we arrive at headquarters." She said. "I'm looking forward to conducting your intake." She said as she made her way towards Santina.

"I want to be a conductor." I heard Santina wine to Nadia.

"Girl," Nadia interrupted her,"You need to stick to what you do best." She said while laughing.

"That's getting this money." Santina replied.

Claudia giggled as she led me down the narrow staircase.

"I told you my homegirls were crazy but you'll see, they are amazingly wonderful as well." She said as she motioned for me to have a seat in the leather recliner. She entered a small door across from where I was seated. Directly across from me were two doors. The first, the door Claudia had entered, had the letters, IHG COO on the front, the other door read IHG CEO. My eyes shifted back to the first door as I heard the knob begin to rattle. The door opened and Claudia stuck her head out. "Come on." she said as she gestured with her hands. I don't know why but I had to take a deep breath just to gather up enough strength to walk towards the door. "Come on, she's not going to bite you. " Claudia said mockingly.

"I was just getting my footing on this moving office." I said as I moved past Claudia and into the office of the IHG COO.

"Hi Rochelle, I'm Julie." she said, extending her hand across her desk.

"Hi Julie." I said Softly.

"Have a seat." She directed. " Actually, can you give me a moment? I will be right back, make yourself comfortable. I just need to follow up with the team about a few things before we arrive at headquarters. I have to start using my professional voice, cause girl listen, excuse me." She said as she closed the door behind her and Claudia.

As I looked around the room, moving from plaques, certificates and awards with my eyes. I felt intimidated. I shrunk a little bit into the leather chair across from such an accomplished woman's desk, where her chair stood tall.

"I'm sorry about that, my apologies." Julie said while entering back into her office. "Claudia is on loan to me this week by our CEO. I have to pull her to the side and ask her things whenever I can because I don't get that much time with her. Miss Rochelle Bampi," she said in a silvery voice. "By now you know that the international homegirls is a discreet and organized group of women with a common mission. We are motivated by hope and the labors of our members. Our goal is to do everything in our power to be able to help shift the paradigm for as many women as possible and to assist them in changing their own individual narratives.

Now I'm getting the answers. I thought to myself. She held my full attention.

She continued. "Our members get a chance to advocate for complimentary membership and high-level membership services for someone identified as in need of our services and can potentially one day, serve as a homegirl. Since we have limited resources, we don't offer many of these types of memberships but you Rochelle Bampi, you were recommended separately by several of our higher-level members and their hand was directly responsible for that emergency homegirl help card mysteriously appearing in your handbag. We knew you would use it when you needed it. I must admit, no one thought it would take you this long before you accepted help."

"Anyway," she continued. "I know you have a lot of questions that will be answered before the day is out but first things first, before you can enter our headquarters, we have a few forms to fill out, saying that you are knowingly and willingly participating in this rescue mission and that no one is forcing you. We need medical records released from your doctor as well." She said.

I looked at her puzzled.

"Just making sure you're still with me." She said. "We don't need medical records but any substance abuse, medical or mental health conditions or concerns should all be disclosed here." She pointed to the area on the document where this was to be completed. I nodded.

"Kenya will hand you a few social media and PR waivers for you to sign and Nadia will have your intake information. Someone will give you the four grand tour and Nadia will make sure that you and Ro get settled in. Trust me," she said, "We all know that this is a lot to take in but we have your and your son's best interest in mind. Everything will make sense soon and we are handling things that you left un-handled on your behalf. All I need you to do is repeat after me." She recited the homegirl pledge and I repeated after her word for word. "Okay looks like we are here, just in time. Let's join the girls up top." She said. We both made our way to the front of the bus .

Tucked away in Chicago's 28th Ward, right off of Madison on a quiet residential block, was the grand embassy like building that was an island all its own.

"What are we doing on this side of town?" I asked. "I mean, why did you decide to put your headquarters right smack-dab, here, I mean?" I inquired. "Why did you choose to build it here?" I corrected myself.

"Do you mean, why we choose to build it here in the hood? As opposed to where, the suburbs? Am I not My Sister's Keeper? Who needs you any less than the drug addicts, prostitutes, the nurses, the teachers that are right here in this community? Surely these women deserve to have home girls too, right?" Said Julie matter-of-factly.

"Oh," I said, " I didn't mean it that way."

"Yes you did." said Julie, "Don't backpedal now. you're only now realizing how classist and elitist and privileged it was for you to assume our headquarters would be in anything less than the perfect location. All due to your preconceived notions about this neighborhood. You'll see a lot more than the struggle if you try." She finished.

We'd arrived to the exit. Santina was standing and helping everyone down the steps. “So check this out,” Santina began to say. “I can take Rochelle on a quick tour and bring her back in time to check in with Nadia.” she finished.

“Sure, Santina.” Julie replied, as she turned to return to her office, I assumed.

“You go ahead .” Said Kenya. “Me and Bug are going to take Roan on his own tour.”

“Okay.” I said. ” Thanks again.” I told her.

“Wait,” said Santina before Kenya could close the bus doors. “She didn’t sign a waiver yet. Is it okay for her to go to the toppity top or do you think she’s going to jumpity jump¿‘she asked looking directly at me.

“I’m fine, I’m not trying to jump off of anything.” I told them.

“Good, you straight then, let’s roll.” Santina said as we stepped onto the sidewalk. “These houses have been lived in by the same families since the 1950s.” She said, pointing to each house individually, she called out the family names. “Miss Smith lived there, Mrs. Williams on the other side, and right smack in the middle was Mrs. Ashford. Legend has it, Mrs. Ashford, was the mother of the founder’s mother. This is the home of our CEOs grandmother, where she and the women in her community raised one another’s children, and provided strong faith-based foundations and moral systems for their families. Many of singing groups were nurtured here. The Story Goes that our founder came to her grandmother’s home one summer to get away from life and that’s when she decided this would be the first International Homegirls headquarters. The neighborhood means a lot to the founder and to IHG and I guess in a way, if you’re going to start saving anyone, it may as well be the community responsible for raising your mother.” She said with unmitigated jubilance.

I couldn’t hide it, I felt her excitement and although I wasn’t in the best of positions I was proud of what they had accomplished and their mission, their mission was everything I needed in life. To be saved and supported by women who wouldn’t give up on me.

“Come on, let me show you around the place.” Santina said as she grabbed my hand and escorted me to the opposite side of the street.

“Are you from this area?” I asked her.” It’s just that you know so much about the buildings of the area." I said.

"No," she replied. "I'm a homegirl. My hometown is Garysburg North Carolina but homegirls travel all around the world and make connections with each community." She finished.

"Man, that's dope." I said forgetting my suburbanite vernacular and substituting it for my more urban mother tongue.

"Indeed it is my sister, indeed it is." She said, patting me on the back and pushing me through the glass doors. "There may be hope for you yet young lady." She said as she turned to face me. With a quick check of her purple leather wrist watch, she grabbed my hand and began to walk to the front desk, indicated by the sign attached to the marble counters standing resolute in the center of the building. "We only have a little time," she advised me, "before I have to get you back to the crew and I have to get on my job job. This place does not pay for itself. It takes money, money, money." she sang.

I laughed. When I heard the sound that had just escaped my lips I found myself frozen. Stuck there reliving the hell Ro and I had just endured

"It's okay." Santina said. " You can laugh sis." She escorted me to the associate at the desk. "Check in for PHRB."she said.

"Oh okay." the associate said, shifting her posture and attention more towards my direction. Her uniform simple but classy, was a plain pink pencil skirt combined with a silk short-sleeve button-up blouse, embroidered with the same logo I found on the glass in the door when I walked in the building. "You're all set, here's your apartment key, your scanner, we have an IHG bag for you to keep any items you may acquire during your stay with us. Here's your lanyard and if you'd give me just a second," she said, " here we go sis. Here's your official pink level International homegirls membership ID card. Try to keep this with you at all times. It has your membership number, emergency numbers, it also is the access card to some of the doors in IHG locations. Lastly, but definitely of the utmost importance, you see this little doohickey on the back of the card?" She said flipping the card over and pointing. " This is a QR code. You need this to access the IHG app and tools. All in which you need during your stay here." She paused. "I think that's it." She said turning towards Santina. "Did I forget anything Santina?" She asked.

"No you did great, I wish I recorded that. It would have been great to upload that on my page. We'd get so many more members if they knew we were as cold as you." Santina said.

"Like Ice Baby." The associate replied. "So I heard about your new homegirl tattoo." She told Santina. "When are you going to let me see it?" She asked her.

"After you finish working." Santina said, tilting her head in my direction, signaling the associate to complete my check in. "Oh I'm sorry." She said.

"That's okay." I replied. " Y'all are too cute."

"As an employee of international homegirls and as a white level member, I would like to welcome you home and we all want you to be aware that we are all here to support you. Do you have any questions?" She asked.

"No, I think I got it." I answered.

"Perfect, on behalf of homegirls everywhere, we hope that entering our doors leads you down the path of living well while doing good." She recited each word with much effort and care. When she was finished, she returned to her original position, towards Santina. "Now you miss thang." She said jokingly. "Don't forget to stop up top tonight. Some of us are opening a vintage bottle of wine that we can't afford near the garden. Plus you still have to show me that tattoo." She announced

"Bet it's a done deal." Santina said with her fist on the desk and the other hand situated inside her pants pocket. She began walking fast, motioning for me to follow her. "All right homegirl, I got to get to this Money!" Santini yelled, as she shot her a wave goodbye.

"She's cute," I said as she held the door open awaiting my entrance."

"Mind your business that's all, just mind your business." She said sarcastically as she followed me into what seemed to be a place of worship of some kind. We both giggled at her sitcom reference but we became quiet as we made our way into the space that she told me was referred to as the Spiritual Center.

"This is where you can come and realign your chakras, talk to God, chant to Yoda, whatever is your pleasure. We don't discriminate. We don't force anything on anyone but we do encourage our members to consult some type of higher power." she said.

"I can dig it." I replied.

" Peace sisters, hey Santina." I heard a fruity voice call from behind us. "I thought that was you." She said.

***

Homegirls Vision

Santina introduced me to Tuyeni. She looked like a brown hibiscus flower, the way her, full natural hair shaped her face. She was a wellness influencer within the homegirl organization and just being around her would make anyone feel better.

They gave me a tour of the conference rooms, the auditoriums, the offices, the artist studios, and the directors offices. There was so much to take in. You could tell that they put a lot of time and effort into every detail of the building. There was an energy moving around the place. Women were moving from place to place, alone, in pairs, and large groups. There were pops of pink and purple in every direction. Just as we made our way from the swag store toward the dinning area, we heard an announcement from the girl at the reception desk.

"Please excuse this interruption homegirls. The time is now noon and all sessions will begin in ten minutes. I repeat, the time is now noon and all sessions will begin in ten minutes. Any new homegirls are required to report to the dining area now. Thank you for your time, Namaste." She said as she ended her announcement.

Santina told me, "Well, looks like you have a session with the boss lady. I'm going to head out and do my thing. You'll be fine with the team."

She walked me over to a table where Patricia and Nadia were already seated.

"Have a seat." Said Nadia.

"Alright ya'll I'm out of here." Said Santina to the group. "Julie, I gave Rochelle over here the four grand tour. You can pay me now." She said.

Julie looked out over her glasses and shook her head as she stood at the front of the room going over the documents sitting in front of her, on the podium.

"I'm going to go do what you pay me for and I'll see some of you tonight on the rooftop." She said pointing to Nadia and Julie. "Not you though, Rochelle." She said. "I'm not sure if we can trust you up there just yet." She finished. "Alright i'm out for real this time." She said, as she exited the dining area.

"I would like to bring this meeting to order." I heard Julie say.

The room became quiet as everyone began to take their seats.

"I'd like to bring this meeting of the the homegirl rescue mission committee to order." Said Julie.

"That's a long name." Said Patricia sarcastically.

I tried not to shift my eyes in her direction. She was beginning to get under my skin. I looked at all the other women in the room with us. Like most of us, these women have at one point found themselves in their own personal hell and crisis.

"Today we have gathered to do what we homegirls do best. To help other women evolve from surviving to thriving. Today we have the opportunity, no the privilege, to rescue two intelligent, strong and powerful women who don't even know how powerful they really are. This is why I come to work." The members were standing on their feet in agreement. It was as if they were the congregation and Julie was the preacher. They were touching and agreeing, her every word.

"We are rescuing you from your crisis. We are giving you your ninth life. We are investing in you so that you can value yourself the way that we do. You will have six days here at the HomeGirl Headquarters. You will learn here, you will eat here, and you will sleep here. You're not here to be babysat. You're here because we only have a short window for you to unlearn your negative behaviors and for you to adopt new ones. We only want you here if you want to be here. If this seems like too much work then you weren't really listening to the words you repeated when you took that pledge earlier." She said with her eyes pointed at Patricia.

"Our six day program is meant to break you down to build you back up. We focus on motivating you to decide what direction you wish to take in life. We help you come up with an action plan then we assist you in executing it." She said. "You have to be your biggest cheerleader here. Do you know how much an organised group of motivated and accomplished women can do?" She asked. "We can change the world." Julie yelled.

"When we started this company, we never thought it would make it this far. Now we're taking private flights to drop in on women in need and employing over three hundred women around the world. We are changing the world." She paused. "We started with one goal in mind. To help our friend be her best self. To help her live in her purpose, design her own lifestyle, and become the narrator to her own story. We did that. Then we did it again and again and again." She repeated. "There is absolutely nothing that we can't do and if you don't believe me now, wait until your last day here." She left the podium to a standing ovation. Even I was standing.

If she could do everything she said she could, I was in. I thought to myself.

We were paired up with our mentors, immediately following Julie's introduction about the homegirl vision. Patricia was given 3 mentors and so was I. In my group was Nadia, Julie, and Dr. D.. I had yet to meet the doctor and Nadia and Julie had to excuse themselves to discuss business. I stood there waiting for instructions. The members held conversation in small groups. I could see Patricia sitting with her mentors. She didn't seem happy but I had only known her for a few hours anyway.

"Hey Homegirl." I heard a familiar voice call from behind me. I turned to see my high-school best friend, walking towards me with her arms stretched out wide, ready to embrace me. "Hey Chelle." She said as she squeezed my arms into my skinny frame.

"Lemon!" I screamed. "Careese, I mean Careese." I said, as we both walked over to grab a table so we could catch up.

"First things first" She said. "How is my friend? I miss you."

Here I was, standing there broken, feeling empty, embarrassed, and sad. It was as if she knew exactly what I needed to hear.

She continued. "We are all the same here." She said. "Whatever you're going through we are all going through with you. I need you to know that I never left you." She finished as she extended her arms and gave me the kind of hug that only she could. A magical hug. God was in her and on her side.

"Have you been to church lately?" She asked.

"You know how it is." I told her. "During our high school years I spent a lot of time in church. Church had become a big part of our life. It's what I learned we did as a family unit. It provided structure. Although conversations detailing the root of why we believed what we believed would end with unanswered questions, we still all participated in this tradition. Being a preacher's kid probably had been the motivation that had also conditioned my mother to keep us in the church and no matter how far away from Black folks and "the city" we were, where you could usually find an inviting community focused congregation, on every other corner, she still made sure to find us a church home where we could be led in our values, morals, and our beliefs molded. When we were back in K-Town, we not only attended a Catholic school but we simultaneously attended First Baptist on 18th and Keeler, where me and my brother were baptized on my 6th birthday. Since Sandy died, my struggles with religion have only gotten worse." I told her.

"Yeah, I heard about that and I saw that you were having a difficult time with her death." She said. "Don't worry, we're going to get through this.

By the end of the two hours we had wrapped up all of our discussions, Nadia returned to introduce me to my third mentor/coach. As soon as I saw her, I thought I was being punked. It was Dr. D.. My Dr. D.. It was Candace from Dream Endlessly. I hadn't spoken to her since the day that the police took me to the crazy house. I felt guilt like I let her down. The first thing she said was, "All is forgiven. Let's focus on the future. We are all here for you."

* * *

It was the end of the night and after finding Roan, Nadia walked us to our room to finally get settled in and take stock of my emotions. Roan was almost asleep when we got to the room. The hotel style suite was clean and sophisticated. It came equipped with a stocked kitchen and let out sofa, which I threw Roan on, right away. As Nadia closed the door behind her, she reminded me not to forget to check the app for my schedule tomorrow.

"I got it." I told her.

"And always remember." She said. "The card is the key." She said as the door shut behind her, leaving me and Roan to fall asleep, finally, alone.

The Breakdown

It was early the next day when my sleep was interrupted by a loud knock on the room door. I jumped up to see who it was. Roan was still asleep and I wanted time before he woke, for myself. To gather my thoughts and try to make sense of everything that had happened in the last two days.

"Rochelle Bampi, let us in." I heard Julie's powerful voice radiate through the hallway door.

"Who do we have to kill first?" I heard a voice say.

I slowly opened the door and peaked my head out. "Why are ya'll so loud?" I asked. By this time, it felt as if we were old friends and they had gained my full trust and cooperation

"You guys are insufferable." I told them.

"We own all of this." Said Santina, as she pushed past Julie and Nadia, making her way into the suite.

I turned back to the three of them, still standing in the doorway.

"Feel free to enter your domain. You own all this any way as your co-worker here has so graciously pointed out." I said sarcastically as they began to walk in, one behind the other.

"You ladies are up early." I said.

"The early worm gets the bag." Said Santina.

"I don't think that's how it goes." I told her.

We exchanged smiles as our attention shifted to the other women standing around the couch.

"How did you sleep?" Asked Dr. D..

"I didn't sleep well at all." I replied. "I kept having nightmares where I was going through different scenarios and in each one , my sister and my father were attacking me." I confessed.

"That is insane." Said Julie. "That sounds like PTSD to me and you're going to need to address that sooner rather than later." She continued. "Sounds like someone needs to start going back to therapy." She laughed. It wasn't a judgmental laugh. More of an endearing, pitiful laugh. I didn't take it personally, coming from her.

"Where is Roan?" She asked.

Pointing toward the closed bedroom door, I told her, "I was tossing and turning so much last night that I just decided to put him in there and close the door. That way he was less likely to hear my screams and I could still be alerted to anyone trying to come in the suite, at the same time." I told them.

"You do know that we pay our security nicely, don't you?" Asked Santina, as she bounced around the room, picking up random items and placing them back down, perfectly. "You're a little extra, huh?" Asked Santina.

"Are you like this with all new recruits?" I asked.

"You can dish it but you can't take it." She said.

"I have no clue what you're talking about." I told her.

"Oh we're going to get to the bottom of it. Don't you pay no never mind." She finished.

"Are you two done?" Asked Julie. "You're worse than my kids, and they are teenagers." She said. "We are here for a reason, believe it or not. We came over this early, not to be rude." She said while looking at Santina, then back in my direction.

"We came to check in on you and Patricia. She's a few doors down from you. We wanted to know if you had familiarized yourself with the homegirl app, and there was something else," she mumbled to herself. "Oh, yeah, and Santina brought you some outfits from our store. We had them sized for you as well. We know that you had to leave everything behind. Some of these I designed and some of these are custom pieces by Shay." Santina said, while holding the clothing up for us all to see.

"Thank you." I told them. "I really can't thank you enough." I said.

"That's right no you can't." Said Santina.

"You can go now." Said Julie.

"I was on my way out the door anyway." Replied Santina.

She sat the bag of clothing on the desk as she made her way to the door.

"One last thing." She said. "Make sure you check her app and make sure she's properly connected before you leave, please." She told Nadia.

"No problem." Said Nadia. "It's handled."

Santina shot her a wink and closed the door as she walked towards Patricia's room.

"Now that the spoiled brat is gone." Said Nadia. "We can go over a few details with you." She said. "We don't want you to be worried about any financial obligations or legal obligations. At least, not while you're here. We are making some moves to set your finances straight and to eliminate the debt you've accrued over the years." She said. "It's so much debt." She said. "What were you doing, girl?" She asked. "Never mind. Don't answer that." She finished.

I could breathe a breath of fresh air. *If what she was saying was true, she was giving me a real new start on life. Not only for me but for Roan.* I thought to myself.

"So how did the app work for you?" Candace interrupted.

"I downloaded it before bed but I really didn't have time to play with it yet." I confessed.

"Well pull it out. Let's see it. When you're provided with tools, you must first learn how to use them." She said. "You don't know, this thing could've told you that you won a million dollars last night but you wouldn't know it because you let someone give you something that was supposed to begin to benefit you today and it's today and you still don't have a clue how to operate the thing." She seemed upset. "We have an hour before breakfast starts. Why don't you and Roan get ready and I'll show you how to use the app on the way to breakfast."

"Actually." said Julie. "We're going to be out and make our next stop before breakfast. We'll let you two work on your little project."

"That sounds like a plan." Nadia said as they made their way towards the door. "See you at breakfast hun."

With Candace and I, left to our own devices, we opened the homegirl app and began to explore. Candace was showing me all of the app features, how to sync my calendar, making sure I had access to the right groups and making certain that I knew where any assignments would be listed. Once she was satisfied that I had learned the app, we got Roan dressed and made our way to the elevator.

As we made our way to the dining area, we saw a group of women returning from walking or running. They were all wearing matching jackets. I could tell that Roan was amazed by the site.

"You should get a jacket like that one day." He told me. "Maybe I will." I replied. "Breakfast was sponsored by Creations by Careese." Announced the woman at the front of the room. "She did an excellent job and we're all very proud of her." She said.

I was proud of her. Although it was bittersweet because I was in the middle of my hell while she was already arrived in Heaven. I found myself slightly uncomfortable, oozing with jealousy.

Before we could begin to partake in our meal, there was a request for the food to be blessed.

"I'll do it." Said Tuyeni.

She stood as silence covered the room.

There were so many homegirls. Each one grabbed the hand of another. I grabbed Roan's hand on one side of me and Candace's on the other. As everyone began to close their eyes and bow their heads, I took the chance to steal glimpses at the women in the dinning area with us. All of them were dressed in their monogrammed sweaters with their pink and purple handbags and notebooks. They were from all walks of life. Each one a different shade of human but together they resembled more of an army. An army I was starting to want to join.

As Tuyeni finished her blessing, complete with Ashe' at the end, we all begin to talk and wait for the meal to be served. There were women coming up to the table to say hello and thank you to Julie, once she and Nadia arrived. There was music playing, lightly, in the background. A perfect sound to increase our Theta waves.

Careese was back at our table now, looking for a place to put her purse. When a passer by pulled her toward them. I heard, "This meal you prepared is delicious and gorgeous. Make sure you link with me on the app. I have several events I'd like you to cater." She said.

"Of course, it would be my pleasure." Careese replied.

As the lady walked off, she yelled back. "Don't forget, the card is the key." She said.

"I won't homegirl." Careese replied.

"You did do a really good job with the food and the decorations." Said Julie to Careese.

"Thanks, Julie." She replied.

"Honestly, I think we should serve a more vegan friendly menu." Said Tuyeni. She was now sitting at the table with us. As the meal courses were flying on the table, we all immersed ourselves in the conversation. "It's a known fact that what we were taught in school isn't applicable to all people and we need to know the truth about each food we put into our bodies." She continued. "I just think there is enough evidence for us to strongly consider promoting a more vegan lifestyle within our organization." She said.

"Normally, I wouldn't have a problem with that." Said Nadia. "But Julie hates vegetables and if you try to give her one, she'll throw it at you." She Said.

"That's right." Replied Julie. "We can educate people on wellness and healthy diets but I feel that we are in no way an authority on the subject. We know women in crisis. I think we should stick to what we know." She finished.

"And as usual, Julie has the final word." Called out Santina from the end of the table, imitating a game-show host.

Julie could tell by the look on my face that I was intrigued by the conversation.

"What do you think Rochelle?" She asked me.

With all eyes on me, I placed my fork on the table and answered.

"I have followed Dr. Sebi's alkaline teachings for years but its difficult for me to make the transition. I've been living with family members and didn't really have the power nor the money to completely do away with the foods that we eat for convenience. I think a mandatory re-education in nutrition is necessary for all of us. We need to realize that everything we were told wasn't true and most of the items that we find in the store, on the shelves, are harmful. After we recognize that, we can all make informed decisions on what we want to eat. Until we get there, this place will continue to run rampant with disease and illness." I said.

"Well look who decided to join the breakfast talk." Said Santina. "Cheers to Rochelle." She said. They all raised their glasses. "Cheers to Rochelle and her Breakdown that's coming up in a few hours." She took a sip then everyone at the table followed her lead.

"The way that sounds, I don't know if I want to even know." I said.

"You'll either hate it or love it." Said Candace.

She was right. There weren't many ways that this could go. I'd either like the process, whatever it was. Or I'd hate it. Either way, I had already agreed and it was too late to turn back now. Leaning away from Roan, I turned to ask Candace a question.

"Is everyone here, a women who you had to rescue from crisis?" I asked

"No." She answered. "Some are entrepreneurs who needed mentors. Some are women who wanted to work in the support industry. Some are though. Some of the women you see here, yes, we did rescue them from crisis and one by one we built this." She said. Her eyes were dancing across the faces of the women in the room. "Some of us take off of work to be here. Some of us, this is our work." She said. "We make this service that we provide a priority." Candace finished.

"Thanks." I said. "For that bit of information."

"You're welcome." She said. "You know the kids at the school miss you and they thought you were a great mentor." She said. "Now all we need to find out is if you're really a homegirl or not." She said. "What's the key?" She asked.

"The key to what?" I replied.

"Are you a homegirl Rochelle?" Santina yelled from her end of the table.

"I don't think she's ready to see this through." She said.

"Leave Rochelle alone y'all." Kenya said as she approached Roan.

"Can we take Roan out after lunch today?" She asked.

"Sure you can." I told her. "He really enjoys hanging with you two. I usually am the only person that he wants to be around. It's good to have friends." I said. "I've always wanted Roan to have a community he felt he belonged to." I finished.

"Well he's got one now." She said.

* * *

It was after lunch when Patricia knocked on my door.

"Do you want a mimosa and to play some connect four?" She asked.

"Sure, why not?" I said as I opened the door to let her in.

"You don't like me do you?" She said, handing me a frozen drink in a pouch.

"What makes you say that?" I asked her.

"Because I always see you rolling your eyes or your face smashed in and nose turned up, every time I say something."

"What if that's just my face?" I said.

"Boo, it's not." She replied. "I see how you talk to the other women. The Black women." She said, placing air quotations around the phrase.

"So you consider yourself White?" I asked her.

"I don't know what I consider myself. All I know about my father is that he had some Black in him. I don't know how much. But to answer your question, yes I do mostly identify as White. Why does that matter?" She asked.

"It doesn't matter, Patricia." I said. "I just needed to understand why you separated yourself from the Black women when you said that I talk to them differently. I don't think I considered you as White. Maybe not fully Black but I wasn't over here counting your drops." I said.

"So we're cool?" She asked.

"Yeah girl. I have other shit to worry about other than you right now. Girl we good." I told her.

"Where is that cute boy of yours?" She asked.

"You mean my little king?" I asked her. "He went swimming with Kenya and her daughter. She and him have become inseparable." I said.

"Speaking of swimming, there's a pool party tonight on the rooftop. It was on my schedule today. Check your app and see if you have the same schedule." She directed me.

I checked my phone. I saw today's agenda and she was right.

"I have the same schedule." I told her.

"Cool. At least I will have someone to talk to." She said. "They act a bit too much like sorority girls." She said.

"And what's wrong with sorority girls?" I asked. "I'm in a sorority." I said.

As she took another long sip of her drink, she shook her head. "You look like a sorority girl." She said.

"The nerve." I said.

Just as I was about to give her a piece of my mind, there was a knock at the door.

"Delivery!"

"What is it?" Asked Patricia.

"Looks like a bathing suit and instructions on how to get up to the roof." I told her.

"I'm going to go to my room and check and see if they sent me one. Meet you at the elevator so we can go up together?" She said.

"Yeah that's cool. I'll wait for you at the elevator because I have to go do all kinds of shaving before I put this bathing suit on." I told her.

I waited by the elevator for twenty minutes before I knocked on her door.

"Are you going to the pool party?" I asked her, shouting through the door.

I heard her moving around inside. I knocked again. "Patricia, open up." I called out.

"I don't feel well." She yelled back.

"Do you need something?" I asked her.

"Just some sleep." She replied.

I figured she'd had too much to drink and needed to sleep it off.

"Okay Pumpkin." I called out. "I will come back to check on you later." I told her.

I made my way to the rooftop with the homegirls.

The outside area was stunning. There was a garden, a yoga studio, a bar, and an art studio. I walked over to where the ladies were surrounding the pool.

"Hello everyone." I said.

"Hey Rochelle." Nadia replied.

I could tell that they were in the middle of a serious conversation.

"Is the other one not coming?" Asked Nadia.

"I knocked on her door but she said she needed to rest because she didn't feel well." I said.

"That's fair." Said Nadia. "One of you go and check on her in a little." She instructed.

"Here, sit down." She said.

I sat on the edge of the pool.

"Here you go." Said Santina. She was handing me a tall glass, filled to the rim with what I could only assume was alcohol.

"You all are really yourselves around one another?" I asked them.

"As opposed to what?" Replied Santina.

"That's funny." I said. "That sounds like a reply I would have." I told them.

"Tell us why you ended up fighting with your family Rochelle." Said Careese.

It hit me harder that she was the one asking the questions that were so personal and sacred. Only because I had known her the longest and had been closer to her than any other member there. I was embarrassed.

I explained how I had lost control. I was honest about the part I played in my own destruction.

"At least you've reached a place where you can be honest with yourself."

Said Careese.

"Do you know who voted for you to become a member, Rochelle?" Asked Julie.

"Careese and maybe Candace?" I responded.

"And me." Said Santina. "You probably don't remember this, but, when you used to be on the downlow website, you and I were friends. I've always had your back." She said.

"Add me to that number." Said Tuyeni. "I never met you but I'm your Soror and we both were initiated into the same chapter and I had to learn your history." She saluted me. "Respect big sis." She said. We went around the pool. Each woman telling me where we've once crossed paths, "I hosted their children during an event." Said Julie. Blown away by their connections to me, I began to cry. Tears were streaming down my eyes as I vented.

After the venting session was over and it was time for dinner, we made our way to the locker room inside the yoga studio. My eyes were bloodshot from all the crying I had just done. As I looked in the mirror, I couldn't help but continue to cry. The image of myself with my thinning hair was all the more confirmation that I did, indeed, look like what I had gone through. As Nadia put on her clothes next to me, she began to speak.

"You fucked up. Why didn't you tell anyone?" She asked. When i didn't answer she continued, "Today you start therapy again."

"And today is your breakdown day, you're allowed a few of those in your life." Nadia Said.

We got dressed and met at the bar.

"I hope everyone likes dinner, it's vegan friendly today." Said Careese.

As soon as she said that, we all burst into laughter.

"See look what you did Tuyeni." Said Santina.

"Tonight we're trying to get some yoga in or nah?" Asked Tuyeni.

"I think you should bless us with a piece." Said Santina.

"Here these two go." Said Julie.

"Here we all go." Said Nadia.

We all gathered into the yoga room. We began to stretch and breathe in, deeply.

As the group began to situate ourselves on the floor, she began:

"When I talk to white people, I change my voice to seem less aggressive. Less intimidating. Less of who I really am. I use terminology foreign to my native tongue but more acceptable to the audience in front of me. A voice that doesn't imbue fear. I say the word "Like", a lot, like way too much to describe but I know this is the language they speak so I switch my vocabulary for their comfort.

As an adult, I've learned that White people are just as messed up as we are. They shop at discount stores while we shame one another for not having the latest name brands. The only difference is they've had four hundred years to assimilate, write the standards for society, and perfect implementation of the formula to keep their world spinning. They became the axis and we the disparate continents of Pangea

As our ancestors lived a life that inspired no motivation to conquer other lands, utilize humans as their unpaid labor force, rape helpless women and men, and never felt such inspiration that would compel them to separate blood relatives from one another simply to lace their pockets with worthless pieces of paper, quantifying the moments of the lives of others, which was only profiting for the makers of standards, operations, and policies; The makers of the laws that govern these lands.

If I hear one more adult say, "slavery was a long time ago, you should get over it and work to make something for yourself. Black people are poor because they're lazy," I'm going to literally, figuratively, and very loudly, scream "SHUT THE FUCK UP" in my deepest, loudest, Blackest voice that I can muster up at the time of said occurrence.

Do they not understand that their entire existence is thanks to us, Black American, Black Africans stolen, removed from their lands and families, tortured on vessels of death, transported to bidding blocks, stripped of their native tongue, deities, belief systems, and history. Everything they have is because of us. When you couldn't bear the heat of your sun you plucked my ancestors with their natural sunblock from their huts and mansions to pick your seeds only for you to reap what they sowed. Oppressed at every turn, we still emerged like seeds grown in darkness. Give us a mustard seed and we will give you mustard greens.

Plucked from their native land, our ancestors were subjected to hundreds of years of DE-humanizing conditions and treatment. The effects of our ancestor's plight is engraved in our DNA. Our bodies were not our own. Owned and sold like cattle, our ancestor mothers learned to keep their heads down, stay in their place, say yes ma'am, yes sir so that the race would not be lost to the world. What they endured is incomparable to anyone's plight. No one endured the levels of oppression forced upon my ancestors for as long as my people.

After slavery, our ancestor mothers had learned to assimilate to more European standards of living. Lost were our belief systems, Lost were the natural herbs utilized to save the ungrateful descendants of the terrorist, by the breast of our mothers . They'll never admit it but their very existence is a direct result of our blood, tears, and breast milk.

As more and more generations adopted this way of living, we lost so much of who really are as a people. Fathers forgot how to be fathers, villages forgot they were responsible for the rearing of future generations, we lost knowledge normally passed down from generation to generation, The offspring became the culturally uninformed. Allow me to vent for a moment. Removing my ancestor mothers from their native land, stripping them of their humanity, outlawing their native tongue, and not allowing them to come together affected not only our ancestors but it affected me.

I know you're like, "you're like 500 years removed from the oppression of slavery, how can you be affected." Let me explain. I've been taught to keep my head down, not to make trouble for myself, and my hair is not good enough. Speaking of hair. Do you know that my sisters in love are only now in 2017 learning how to care for their hair, bodies, mind and souls because our ancestors were too busy trying to keep Mister off of their daughter to teach us the ways of our people. In our community, the darker you were meant maybe you could escape a night of brutal rape.

Removed from our natural habitat, like a fish on land, we survived but what a price that was paid. Yeah, I'm still learning about the wonders of the flourishing natural gifts given by our native land that made us such a valuable people with valuable real-estate. I now know the joys of shea butter and coconut oil. I'm four generations removed from slavery. This means that there were three women before me that never learned how to maintain their natural hair and that tried to appear more European because it was an easier way to exist. No one taught them the natural remedies of our people, which means no one taught me. This made us a lost people. A people without a home, without a land. Our ancestor mothers were bred like the mules used to plow the lands of slave owners by our ancestor fathers, brothers and sons.

One resource provided was the introduction of the internet. Thank you, Our community is slowing recovering from your foot on our throats.

Black girls, Black women, we fight so many fights at once. We've lost or abandoned our culture for a more accepted way of living. We are existing, some of us are still walking around with our heads down, eyes low, and lost. It's time to come home. We are the ancestor mothers for the next generations and we are responsible for the progression of our people. We are here now and it is up to us to decide that no longer will we allow the ramifications of slavery (ending only to some in 1865 as a direct result of The Thirteenth Amendment), Black Codes, a rigged period of Reconstruction, Jim Crow and poverty following the Civil War, White Supremacists in the KKK (Ku Klux Klan), the Compromise of 1877 leaving the descendants of African lands unprotected with no troops to enforce the Fourteenth and Fifteenth Amendments, providing little to no resources for the newly free, providing New Deals where the only ones that sat at the table to bring forth such a deal, didn't look like and had never experienced the form of oppression of the people who were to benefit from such a deal. News flash, they didn't benefit. They were housed in project buildings, after greatly migrating from the world of sharecropping and brutality.

We were set up to fail. We didn't but there is so much left to do. Before I leave this Earth, I had to tell you that it is now up to you my sisters to become the ancestor mothers of today. We pay homage to the blood shed by our ancestors by taking their place and recognizing our responsibilities. Yes, we are still recovering. Yes we are still suffering. Yes, some of us if not but a few, are suffering from (PDS) POST DRAMATIC SLAVERY. We have become the incubators of depression. We fight our first mind to brace for the impact of theirs.

I have felt the hardships and pains of the women who came before me. If it hurts today, It must have felt like Hell on Earth 400 years ago. So to the ones that says "let's just get over it," watch how we get over it and be ready to fall back because this is ours. You're here because we allow it. Never forget.

Everything in society served as an incubator to my insecurities. It's already hard enough to be a human. You have to learn to feed yourself, provide shelter, and protect yourself at all times. Whose idea was it to make life so much more difficult for the Black and brown girl? Now not only must you survive but you also must learn to protect yourself from anyone and everyone. Those who look like you and those who don't.

Those who come from distant lands with different tongues and regurgitated versions of the God you know as your own, (because you know that its okay for people to pray to their own God, it's all theory anyway and no one here on earth is equipped enough to offer validity to any one theory). Those that force you to speak a broken version of their tongue, those that take you away from all your shea nut, your gold and diamonds. Those who would change the men of tribal warfare to senseless murderers.

Those who would come to kill the wisdom hoarded by our ancestors so that it could be replaced by their watered down way of life and thinking to our ancestor's descendants. For those among you who would dare taint your soul then strike you for having a tainted soul. For those who would cut our hair where we would later trace our way back to our birth rights. For these reasons are the reasons you must know who you are." She said. "Namaste."

* * *

Ancestor Mother

Women who were Earth and Mother, Queen to us all. Her children recognized her strength, beauty and her wisdom. The Mrs. Pattons, The Grandma Mildreds, the Big Mammas, and the My dears. How did you survive? Being stolen? Forced to labor. Forced to be in labor. Burned bodies put out on display. Learned to quiet your loud tone over the centuries to see to the continuity of Your people. Took up bed with danger to protect your children and their children's children. We are the children of their children. Ancestor Mother who had her language systematically removed, was warned not to try to learn to read or write in this new land. You became a poet, Ancestor Mother.

Motivation

After yesterday's festivities, all I wanted to do was sleep until noon. I heard the alarm blaring from my phone on the nightstand. I reached over to hit the snooze as Roan's elbow appeared from under the blankets.

"I thought I put you in your own bed." I said out loud.

It was motivation day and although I still had my reservations, I was open to trying things there way. I was trying not to think about my family and my messed up life.

I opened the app to look at my schedule only to find that they expected me to participate in some kind of boot camp. Motivation camp the schedule read. It was almost 6:00 in the morning. I tiptoed around the room, grabbing my jogging pants and jacket from the bag Santina gave me yesterday. I crept out of the room and into the bathroom without making a noise. As I slid the pajamas off, supplied also by your friendly International Homegirls, I began to have a conversation with my thoughts.

I don't want to live like this anymore. I thought to myself. *I want so much more out of life, too much to let life beat me. I owe it to Roan to win this fight. He didn't ask to be here and he deserves so much more. Whatever we're going to be, we need to decide now and stick with it. We need a plan. Whatever these women have to offer, let's receive it. We don't want to fail anymore.*

In agreement with my inner thoughts, I took my time to get ready for the day's boot camp session. I stood in the mirror, trying to make the best out of what I had to work with. I plucked hairs from my face, squeezed and scrubbed the white heads from my skin, and placed oils on the edges of my hairline in a last attempt to stimulate growth. I made myself happy with the image I saw reflected back to me.

"I'm okay and Roan is okay and I have support." I told myself.

With a last gaze in the mirror, I flicked the light switch and strutted towards the kitchen to grab a water. I went over, in my head, the activities and assignments for the day. I had a meeting with Nadia after breakfast and again after lunch. From the short time that we had already spent together, I knew that she was going to be sisterly, but straight forward too. I knew that it was up to me to be mentally prepared.

I reached the door just in time to open it before Kenya could attempt her third knock.

"Good morning ladies." I said as Kenya and Bug waddled into the room. Wrapped inside of their blankets, each one still in her pajamas, were holding pillows in their arms.

"We came to watch Roan." Kenya said in between her yawns.

"Looks like somebody stayed up too late last night." I said.

"This one wanted to practice her cheer-leading routine all night." replied Kenya.

Bug and I smiled at each other as Kenya walked over to the couch and sat down.

"Go handle your business Miss Rochelle." She said. "We'll be here when you get back." She said as she turned on the television.

"Bug come over here and watch TV with me." She said.

"Alright, bye y'all." I said.

"Motivation will die. You have to learn discipline." Careese was shouting as we ran around the track, across the street from headquarters.

"I'm about to die. That's who's going to die." I said as the other women passed me by, for the third time.

"Remember that time you tried to run track?" Careese asked.

Bending over to catch my breath, I stood next to her as she kept an eye on the real runners.

"First of all, why would you even bring that up?" I asked with staggered breaths.

She let out a hefty laugh.

"I forgot to eat." I explained.

"That was your excuse but that's not what happened." She replied.

"I thought I could run but I forgot that you can't stop for breaks when you're running a race." I told her.

"So you fainted." She said as she continued to laugh.

"It's not that funny Lemon." I said sternly.

"Yes it is, Babygirl. Yes it is."

Grateful for the break in between laps, I walked along her side as we remained in the slow lane, circling the track.

"How are the girls?" I asked.

"Hadija and Ebony are both doing well" She answered.

"It's been a long time since the four of us were together." I said.

"Yeah we're all old and married with kids now." Careese said.

"Y'all are married, old, with kids." I snapped back.

"I don't think I'll ever be married." I told her.

"You don't know what you want anyway." She said. "One minute you're with a woman and the next you're with a man. You need to pick a struggle." She said.

"You know I missed you until you turned into a wise drill sergeant." I said.

"Remember that time you fell coming out of my parents house that time and my dad called my ass at college to laugh about it?" I asked her, subtly shifting the subject.

We both laughed.

"You know Rochelle, you've been through a lot and everyone understands that but what you do with your life now is totally up to you. There are a lot of us that want to see you win. The world isn't out to get you and in all fairness, you've been wishy washy since junior high." She said. "You start something, you don't finish it. I know you have the best intentions but I need you to promise me one thing." She said. "I need you to promise me that you're not going to give up on yourself and that you'll see this through.

I promised her.

"Okay I want three laps around the track." She blew her whistle and sprinted ahead.

After finishing my laps, I couldn't wait to get a shower. We made our way to the dining area after we were dressed. Kenya and Bug had arrived moments earlier and had saved us both a seat. I was starving from this morning's run and wasn't any good for conversation. I had so much on my mind. I found it difficult to stay focused and the time for my meeting with Nadia was quickly approaching.

* * *

"Did you find the classroom easily?" She asked

"To tell you the truth, no. No I did not." I replied.

"The building is crazy." I said. I walked around for an hour before I found my way. you guys even have an indoor gazebo. Why do you have an indoor gazebo?" I asked.

"Girl I don't know, it's something that Julie probably ordered online she does that a lot." Said Nadia.

"How was your morning running with Careese?" asked Nadia

"It was okay." I replied. "It's been a while since I ran. It felt good just to clear my head." I told her.

"Yeah running can be therapeutic." she responded. "And you could use a little therapy. Did you do all the laps?" She asked.

"Yes, I ran them all and just about damn near died." I said.

"That's good that you didn't give up and that you didn't die." She said.

"Anything that you desire from this world, you can have Rochelle." She said while looking me straight in my eyes. "You only fail when you stop fighting." She said.

"I think I'm done with giving up on myself." I responded.

"Good because you still have a lot of fight left in you. We don't want it to go to waste." She finished.

"No we don't." I responded.

"You know that I always come with questions." Said Nadia. "My first question for you Rochelle," she went on, "is what do you want to be when you grow up?" She asked. "What is it that you see yourself doing?" She asked. "Yesterday, you were a puddle of tears explaining how you got to this point in your life. I want you to realize that from this moment on, that part of your life is over. You get to decide the next moments and the next ones after that. What are you going to decide for yourself?" She asked. "At some point you must take control. You must decide that the way you once lived your life is no longer the way that you will choose to experience life. Have you made that decision?" She asked.

"Yes." I replied.

"Fine. Now we can move forward." Said Nadia.

"I don't really know if I see myself as just being one thing or having one purpose." I told her. "I'm a jack of all trades." I said.

"You may be able to perform many tasks but that doesn't mean you're the best at everything you do." She replied.

"I used to just go with the flow and try to find a path or a place where I fit in before I had Roan. Now I can't do that. I have to pick one direction to go into and stick with it. I've messed up so much that starting in a new direction seems unfathomable." I told her.

"Well you're not dead." She said. "So you can still make it out of here okay." She said. "You still have to have a purpose while you remain here. You just can't give up on life."

We were sitting in the classroom, the two of us, and her attention was solely upon me. She sat behind the desk and pulled out a binder from her briefcase.

"Rochelle." She said. "While you're here at headquarters, you have to decide what path you're going to choose. No one can choose besides you. You know that you don't have to worry about anything financial but the decision of where you and your son are going to end up, are in your hands.

I don't know how much more motivation you need besides all of us here telling you that we're behind you and that your and your son's life depends on you making this journey."

Everything she was saying was true. She was tugging on heartstrings that I had pushed deep down inside and steered clear from for the past few years of my life. It was time to make a decision and stick with it. Wherever we would end up at least I'd give it a try.

"I want to use my life experiences to help other women overcome their fears of living as their authentic selves." I told her. "I want to help other women restore their natural hair as I am attempting to restore my own. I want to give them their power back as well as their beauty." I tried not to stumble on each carefully chosen word as I knew each word was a promise that I was now making.

"If that's what you want to do, we can work with that. just let me get a couple things together and I will be back to you. Meet me back here after lunch. Bring your notebooks and pens and we'll get down to work." She said.

I walked out of the classroom afraid of what was to come. As I made my way back to the fourth floor, thoughts of Patricia began to flood my mind. I knew that she was supposed to be in session with us but I hadn't seen her since yesterday, before the pool party. I planned to stop by her suite to check on her. Before I could reach her door, Kenya popped her head from behind the door, leading to my room and began to ask questions about my meeting with Nadia. We made our way inside, closing the door behind us.

"How did everything go with Nadia, Rochelle?" Asked Kenya.

"Everything went well except I think I put my foot in my mouth by telling her that I wanted to continue to build my hair care brand that I started earlier this year." I told her.

"I think that's a good idea." She said. "I followed you when you first began creating your natural hair growth serum." She said. "I watched how you created the product and how you posted your tutorials online. I love the way you were naturally marketing and promoting your brand. I thought it was an amazing idea. And I still do. You should definitely do this." She said

"Yeah Mom, you should do it." Said Roan. "Don't let your dreams just be dreams." He added.

"I guess I can't let you down kid." I said. "I'm going to give it a try and see what happens. Hopefully, I've made the right decision." I told them. "I'm supposed to go back to see Nadia after lunch if you don't mind watching Ro again for me." I told Kenya.

"I don't mind at all." She said. "He and Bug have become quite the pair." She said. "They are even starting to sound alike." She finished.

My meeting with Nadia was nothing to play with. She came ready with my new career in a bag. She had options.

"Think about what is going to take to be this." She told me. "We broke you down yesterday so that we could begin the work of building you up today." She announced. "You're a new you now. I want you to think about this and on decision day I want a firm yes or no from you. Is this the road you choose? Don't give me an answer now." She finished.

Hope

The morning routine of working out and breakfast was over. I hadn't seen Claudia since the first day at headquarters. I was surprised to see her when she stopped by to check in with a warning that Julie was a hard ass. She knew that today was the day that I was going to have my one on one and she was there to give me encouragement.

"As long as you remain committed to the cause of saving your own life and you're honest, she's going to be your biggest advocate." She told me.

She suggested that I called on Careese and Tuyeni for spiritual guidance.

I didn't want to talk to anyone about God and I definitely didn't feel as if I needed any spiritual guidance, but I had come this far and I felt as if not calling them would make my situation worse. After talking to them both, I knew that I had my work cut out for me. I felt drained from everything that led me to this point and I wanted to give up. Going to sleep until all of this was over, sounded like a much better plan than going and talking with Julie but I knew that I had to get past how I was feeling.

As I mustered up the courage to meet with Julie, I sat on the edge of the bed going over in my head what I would say to her. The last two days had been filled with motivation, guidance, and real honest woman to woman mentoring. I had never experienced anything like this in my life. I was grateful for them saving me. I was grateful for them providing a safe place for me and Ro but I didn't feel as if I could accomplish what they wanted of me. I was stuck. Just as I began to dwell on the things that I had gone through, as I did so often, I received a notification on my phone from the homegirl app. It was Shay.

I hadn't had time to really go through the app and see everything that was offered and I didn't know why I was receiving a notification from Shay but I tapped on it anyway to reply. She wanted to know if I needed anything. If I was ready for my meeting with Julie and if I had anything to wear. The only clothing I had were the clothes I wore when I arrived and the bag of clothing that was delivered by Santina days ago. I knew I needed something new and something more professional that would garner the respect and sophistication needed to make it through this meeting. As I began to type my response to her inquiry, my phone began to ring.

" Hey it's me Shay." she said. I got your number from the app I hope it's okay if I called you."

"It's perfectly okay." I told her. "I was borderline having a panic attack."

"No worries, lady." She responded. "I'm on my way with options."

When she arrived we tried on outfit after outfit, attempting to find the perfect match.

"It's about time for you to come out of those comfortable clothes because you're going to need to be uncomfortable if you want to overcome." She said.

We tried on pant suits, dresses, and skirts until we finally decided on a pencil skirt and a button-up blouse. we talked about how she herself had endured a crisis in her own life and she gave me a book that she thought I should read.

She said, "Sometimes you need to look within for answers to some of life's most complex situations. Sometimes we find ourselves at various crossroads that require us to make difficult decisions. With every decision, we have to be prepared to accept the consequences."

I was listening to her with open ears. She felt like a sister. Someone I had known my entire life and knowing that she had gone through a crisis of her own but was standing in front of me like nothing happened, gave me hope that I would one day be standing in front of someone, giving them this same feeling of hope. As she left the room she held my hand and squeezed it tightly.

"A homegirl always comes through." She told me as I held back the tears. We said our goodbyes and I made my way down the hall to meet with Julie.

"Good luck with Julie." Yelled Shay as she boarded the elevator.

My hands, drenched with perspiration, began to shake as I turned the knob to open the door that led to her office. Standing four feet ahead, Julie extended her arm and guided me to the chair across from her desk.

"Look at you looking like a professional homegirl." She said. "I'm proud of you for making it this far. The past few days couldn't have been easy for you, especially with a kid. I hope you've had a chance to rest and get ready for this next season of your life. You have to participate in your own revolution, Rochelle. Change the paradigm and you will see your reality change. You cant sit and wait for someone to tell you who you are, why you are or where you should go." She said.

"You know here at IHG we ask a lot of questions because we are trying to save your life in a limited amount of days and no one on this earth has gone to the school of Rochelle repair so you're going to have to bare with me. I only have two for you. Who are you and how do you want to live your life? Before you answer," she said, "I want you to consider what you need to do for yourself, for your son, for your spirit. This isn't about money, although that's a factor. This is about you making room for your gifts to lead you in this life. The rain falls on the just and the unjust. If you're going to be in the rain, you may as well dance." She said. "It's time to change your mindset." She finished. "What is your value to this world?" She asked me. "Let us help you and add value to your life. Value that you don't even know you need."

I was stunned by her words. Why would she put so much time and effort into me? I thought to myself.

"The energy that this will require will make you have doubts but you can't be led by fear. Only focus. What's holding you back from your own success is you. You can't do this half way. You have to go all in or don't play the game. Remove your self doubt. Get a job or a career, do something or what are you here for?" She asked. "You're lazy, you make excuses and you are afraid to live. I hope you make the right decisions for you and that young man."

"Your finances are in shambles, you're basically homeless now, Roan should be in school or receiving a quality education from someone, somewhere and you, you should be a stable provider who can make sure he has what he needs. I understand why you wanted to give up. Why you attempted to leave this Earth but you can't escape this. Not anymore. You have got to face this."

She was behind her desk now, holding a stack of papers.

"These," she motioned, "these are all of your unpaid bills, your student loans, your debt. There is a lot to unpack here but we need to start somewhere. I want you to sit down with Santina and come up with an actual workable plan that you can execute before you leave here in a few days. I want you to be prepared when you get back out there and I don't want to see you ever bring yourself down this far again. The beauty in being a homegirl is that it's our job to see that you win. In every part of your life." She finished.

Embarrassed, I placed my head into the palms of my hands, still covered in the perspiration from moments ago.

"It's okay. Well it's not okay but we are going to get you together." Said Julie. "Are you committed to being financially responsible and to fix this?" She asked me.

I let out a soft, "yes." To which she replied, "Breathe. Right now you're suffocating. I understand why they locked you up. I would have locked you up to. You can't just be out here flying by the seat of your pants. You need structure, morals, values, a code to live by, something to believe in. You're doing this all wrong Rochelle."

She handed me a list of action items to complete and said, "You haven't failed Rochelle. You simply haven't learned how to pass the test yet. Some of us take longer than others but if you really commit to rising out of your downfalls and this situation, you'll come out on top and that's all I want for you. I want to see you make it." She said.

I sat up that entire night. Trying to put my thoughts on paper. I was mind mapping the riddles chanting inside my head. I decided who I was going to be. I wrote it all down. It was the most tedious exercise I'd ever have to do. I was sure that I wouldn't finish the action items in time but somehow I did. I finished every one. I went through my finances and debt with Santina. I prepared myself for the next day where I would be required to tell them all what I had decided. I was going to have to finally answer their questions. I could no longer hide and I knew it. As I shuffled through the papers and uploaded my plan to the homegirl app, I heard a loud commotion going on in the hallway. I opened the door to see what all the noise was.

"She's gone." Said Kenya.

Patricia had succumbed to her battle with alcohol and drug abuse. IHG was on lockdown.

"If we only got to her sooner." Said Santina.

This was it. I made my decision. I was ready. I refused to die. *Not like that and not without a fight.* I told myself.

* * *

Ceremony of Love

You must take your time when you do this. Rub gently every strand. Run your oil kissed fingers to each coil's end. Gently tuck away your coconut loved strands with the finest satin cloths. Free ears from its bondage. Tie in secure know intentionally placed. This is the ceremony before bedtime.

Execution

Patricia's untimely Death was a shock, to say the least. I knew that she liked to drink a lot from our short conversation the night right before the pool party but I had no idea that she would end up dying while everyone was in the middle of trying to save her life. It made me think about things and made me think about who I wanted the world to see me as when I was no longer here. it made me think about what I would be leaving for my son if I hadn't succeeded in anything before I died. We all drink. Some of us smoke. And some of us do other things to dull the pain of living and to not feel when it gets to be too much. I know what that's like. I've been there. I'm there now.

But It's not as if, I desire to be here anymore. Somehow I have got to get around this I told myself. Everyone was tense and there was a chill in the air. It was decision day and considering everything that had happened, it was do or die, in my eyes. I could not dwell on Patricia's passing. Although sad, I had my own life to save.

When Roan woke up he began dancing uncontrollably. I didn't tell him what had happened the night before. I didn't want to spoil his fun. I took his hands in mine and we began to dance together.

" It feels good to be silly us, again." He said. "I haven't thought about being sad, mommy. I'm sorry you had a fight with your family but I'm glad that you have your homegirls." He told me.

"Me too kid," I replied. "I guess this is what living feels like."

I thought breakfast would be quiet. I thought that things would change in the atmosphere but it didn't. It was the same as before. Life was going on. Sitting at the table, I watched as members spoke to one another, some homegirls giving me a head nod and a smile as they went about their business. I knew it was time for me to verbally commit to my decision. After Consulting with Nadia, Careese, Tuyeni, Julie, Kenya, and Shay, I had no more excuses. I called for their attention and began to speak.

" I've made up my mind," I said. "I want to thank everybody for standing by me and trying to make me see that I could live and not be in pain. Thank every one of you for pouring into me the energy that I could not pour into myself. I know that I have a bigger purpose. I know that I'm strong. I know that I have no choice and my strength should never be a weakness."

"I don't have all the answers. And I will never have all of the answers but it is up to me and I know that it is up to me to define the next season of my life. I've learned from you that I need to plan for success. I've learned from you that I need to map out how I'm going to be successful. And this is what I'm going to do. I've decided to continue my journey as an entrepreneur. I'm going to be a businesswoman. I'm not going to care how anyone else feels about it. And I'm going to do it with the best of my ability."

They all began to cheer as I took my seat.

By the evening, I was getting into the middle of the action. I was making calls, asking questions, and making the magic happen. I was totally feeling myself. I had a goal and a purpose. Dr. D was at the door. She said she wanted to help. I had always considered her a friend and I trusted her with my secrets. It was nice to have her around. We talked about our dreams and how difficult it had been for both of us to find our place in the world. How it was difficult for most Black women and how it would be my responsibility to share the powerful message of how sisterhood, mentoring, and guidance can save you from yourself and lead to a better quality of life.

"You control the outcome." She said. "You write the script. You control what characters make it into your movie and you are allowed to make edits along the way."

"You're going to be the face of not only endurance but success and overcoming." She told me.

As we continued to plan and gossip, the parade of homegirls began to fill in the small suite, one by one. Careese came with food, Kenya returned with Roan and marketing materials, Tuyeni came in and set the mood, Shay brought us shirts she designed, and good old Nadia sent a text saying she wouldn't be making it over tonight, she was here in spirit. " I'm going to bed to be the rested half of you tomorrow." She said. Before I could submit the master plan, Candace asked, "do you have the drive to reach the dream?" I pressed send on the action plans and loaded the Financial plan.

I was grateful for their help but it was go time now. I kicked them all out so that Ro and I could get a good night's sleep. We got up early the next day. It was going to be our last full day at IHG headquarters and I didn't want to waste any time. I heard my grandmother's voice, repeating in my mind. "You ain't never supposed to let yourself down Chelle." She'd tell me and she was right.

I submitted all the forms and completed all the steps. Everyone had the plans so what happened next would be up to me. It always has been.

I received a notification from Tuyeni reminding me to get spiritually centered and Careese didn't forget to remind me that although, today was the first day of the rest of my life, I still had to workout. I could tell that they were not going to make this easy for me. I was going to have to work for it.

It was time to execute my plan. We set up a flagship office, equipped with computers, cameras, and the homegirls for staff. Our mission was clear. If we were all using our networks to promote one another, it would increase our reach. They all jumped on social media, added me to their friend lists, and followed the page Kenya and I had created. She was showing me the ins and outs of managing a business. Sure I had some knowledge but she was breaking down processes and techniques that I had never heard of. I was following her directions at every step. The plan was to let my friends, out in the world, know that I needed their support and attention. Once I had everyone's attention, it was my job to inform them about the re-launch of Journey. As soon as I created the posts, I received a notification. A donation for start-up costs was posted. They were listening and responding to my cry. All of them. Women came from everywhere. They called. They emailed. They asked how they could invest, not only into my company but into my future. It was all going so fast. It was surreal.

I could hardly catch my breath when Nadia and Julie approached me.

"You executed the hell out of this." Julie said loudly, stopping everyone in their tracks. "I know you're a bit overwhelmed but we wanted to tell you, everything was set up perfectly. You're actually doing it." She said.

"Honestly, this is the best day of my life." I told Julie. "I feel empowered and ready like I've never felt before. Still afraid but ready."

"Congratulations," Nadia said. "I'm proud of you." She finished.

I thanked her and told her that I was proud of me as well.

"The reality is you go back out in the world tomorrow," Julie said. "You have to be ready." She told me.

"I feel ready. I am ready." I replied.

"Do you know what you are? Do you know what you believe? Do you know how you want to live your life? Do you know what that looks like? Do you know what it's going to take to get there? Do you have the drive to get yourself there? What say you, Rochelle?" Julie was speaking in a soft voice but you could hear a pin drop in that room. I knew that all the women were listening.

She turned to the gathering crowd, asking that they all lean in a bit closer.

"I ask you, members of IHG," she said, "does she have what it takes?"

Unexpectedly, they all began to reply.

"Yes." They said.

"Rochelle Bampi, what are you?" Julie asked.

"I'm a homegirl." I replied.

The room became quiet again. Julie looked around the room and scanned the eyes of each member. "What say you IHG, is Rochelle Bampi a homegirl?" She asked them.

To which they all replied, together, "Yes she is. Hey Homegirl." They said.

The Answer

"The ups and downs of the past week have been insane." I told Nadia. She and Kenya were standing in the doorway, waiting for Roan and I to finish packing all of our belongings. I was still floating on cloud nine from yesterday's events. We totaled over thirty five thousand dollars in investments and pre-sales. They were keeping their promises and had made sure that Roan and I would have some security. I was reluctant to leave them but I knew that they were just a notification away.

"Julie had to return to Florida but she left detailed instructions for you. She's so proud of you. We all are." Kenya said. We exchanged information and set up playdates for the kids. Then we made our way downstairs for our last breakfast, homegirl style.

"You can open that up later." Said Nadia, handing me a small black envelope. "It's from Julie." She explained. "Do you still have that bag of clothing that Santina gave you?" She asked.

"I do." I replied. "Did you want it back?" I asked.

"No, that is yours to keep. There was a small scanner at the bottom of the bag. Did you find it?" She asked.

"Oh that's what that was." I said, smiling. "I'm old. I never know what these new gadgets are." I told her.

"Grab that scanner, you'll need it after breakfast." She instructed.

"What am I scanning?" I asked her.

"You'll see." She replied with a smirk and a smile.

"I think I should be worried." I mumbled.

"What's new?" She shot back. "You know, Julie and I wondered if we would need some extra help with you, after that first day. We were a little worried but you pulled through okay, didn't you?" She said.

"I did, didn't I?" I replied confidently.

Careese prayed over breakfast and Sarina, someone I recognized from my childhood, served us her popular cake-pops. We made vows and commitments. As we were leaving breakfast Claudia approached our small, yet bonded group of homegirls.

"Did it happen yet?" She asked.

Tuyeni interrupted her. "No, so be quiet." She told Claudia.

"What's going on?" I asked them, puzzled by their whispering. "Is this a yoga session before y'all put me back out there in the big bad world?" I joked.

"No, we are going to visit Shay." Said Tuyeni. "Come with us homegirl." She demanded.

We all walked around the headquarters, for what was to be my last time. As we approached the homegirl swag store, Nadia stepped in front of me and said that I should wait.

"You can open it now." She said.

I had forgotten all about Julie's letter and I was sure that whatever was inside was going to be motivational but I was hesitant to open it and read it in front of everyone. Nadia noticed.

"Girl if you don't open that letter, I will!" she said

Dear Rochelle,

After working with you the past few days we had a meeting to review your progress. Patricia's departure really threw us. It made us re-evaluate how we do what we do.

You are a special case and you need special handling. You need to get your life together but without adequate help on the outside you won't get the work done that you need to complete on the inside. So, we are prepared to help you with the following:

1. You and Roan may remain at HQ for six months. You will enroll him at World Academy beginning on Monday. We have arranged for his records to be transferred already.
2. Roan will also attend an after school program that includes STEM, sports/fitness, social skills, language development and therapy.
3. You will commit to continuing the plan you have worked out with our members and mentors. All resources, including investors, will be provided for you. You will have to win them over but we will pave the way for you.

In addition, it means following the rules we have laid out for HQ:

1. No overnight guests;
2. No smoking, drinking or illicit drugs;
3. Keeping all therapy and doctor appointments as arranged for and by you;
4. We are not babysitters and you will be a full-time mom to Roan. He will be safe here on the few occasions that you will have to be out in the evening for your business but do not expect it otherwise.
5. You and Roan will be responsible for your own laundry, care of your living quarters to our standards and following the schedule set at IHG HQ for all participants.

Rochelle, you have an opportunity here to help us plan the future of IHG. Consider this an experiment that is open to re-evaluation as needed but will be directed by us. At all times, if there is a disagreement with our process, you are free to leave and do it on your own. But we don't half-step and neither will you.

You will have to accept this agreement within 24 hours of its receipt in person in my office. There are more details to be figured out but if you are willing, so are we.

Sincerely,

Julie

I looked up at Nadia, my eyes filled with tears. "I can't believe that she, you," I pointed at her, then to the women, "and all of you, would take the time that it took to do all of this for me and my kid." I told them.

"Now go be a powerful force and remember you deserve this." She said. "One day you will be in a position to do this for someone else. When you do, make sure you tell her that the homegirls sent you." She added. "Now let's go on this shopping spree she said."

"Shopping spree?" I replied.

"Yes, homegirl. When Julie said we were going to set you up, she meant that." Said Santina. "All you have to do is walk in there, scan items you would like, and they will all be delivered. It's that simple." She finished.

"This is all too much." I told them.

"This is God's plan." Said Careese.

I scanned and cried. Roan was all set up. I was all set. We had everything we needed and more. We had a goal, a plan to accomplish the goal, a support system, and a bright future ahead. There was no more looking back. I was only looking forward.

Settling into our temporary home, back in our old suite, Roan and I danced around the bedroom until we heard a knock at the door.

"Open up." I heard her shout from the other side of the door.

"Is everything alright?" I asked her.

"Yeah, I just wanted to stop over and say my goodbyes to you and my nephew." She explained. "And to make sure that you stay off of the rooftop without proper supervision." She said jokingly.

"You really are too much Santina." I told her. "You've made me laugh and kept my spirits up this entire time."

"Not the entire time, but I know what you mean." She replied.

"Come in." I told her.

"I'm glad that everything has worked out for you." She began.

"I'm glad that we found you in time for you to be saved. Do you know how many women succumb to their own depression, anxiety, and fears simply because they were alone or felt alone in this world? You helped us save you and for that I'm proud of you." She continued. "As a child I endured pain that many of us should never witness. However, it is a big issue within our society." She said.

"For years I would dream of some hero, appearing out of nowhere, but just in time to break me free from the pain I carried. Each time he tied me with a belt and allowed me to dangle in his closet, I would scream and cry for help because I knew what was next to come. No one ever answered." She explained.

We were sitting on the couch now. I held back showing my surprise at her confession, as she continued.

"No one batted an eye when they saw how internally and externally I was bruised. The pain leaked from my soul to the extremities of my body from being battered by a boy who was supposed to be my cousin. My family. I suffered for years. When the darkness overpowered me, as he forced my head into the bed, snatched my pants down, and shoved himself inside of me, I screamed for a savior as if they could hear me. I would twist, turn, and fight with every inch within me. Each and every step, I began to melt away. The person I was meant to be in this world no longer seemed plausible. Broken, weak, and unable to know what happiness actually was. I didn't understand the pain that I was carrying on my shoulders. In search of love and a sense of belonging, I wandered aimlessly in a world that was not meant for me. I leaned on friends for companionship and a sense of connection. I had no family." She explained.

"Though I built a family of friends in the military, I was still roaming aimlessly and I fell in love with a woman because I wanted to be loved and nurtured. But then she just took what was left of me away. It was like what I wanted didn't ever matter to anyone. I was just a target for a narcissistic woman who said her love was real. It was like being under water all the time. As I laid there under water, I saw my life slip away and all my dreams drifted away in the darkness. I was ready to give it all up because I just knew that this world was not meant for me." She said.

"Eventually my hero showed up. I began to speak to myself in a manner that only I could interpret. The passion and love that came from within made me rise from the water. I began to piece myself back together like I was a broken vase. I loved me more than any person in this world could ever love me. I started to clean the toxicity out of my life. I thoroughly understood how this world may not be for me but I am here to learn the human form, so I can reach my next journey. It took 31 years to find my hero. I had always dreamed that one day someone would come save me. I never knew I would save myself." She finished.

"You know you just got really deep for like the first time since I met you." I told her.

"And if you tell anybody, I'll cut you." She joked.

"What happened to the you that I met a week ago?" Asked Santina.

"Shit, she had to die, so she could live." I replied.

"I'm glad she didn't jump off the roof though, because you know, they told me you were nuts, so I was just very concerned for your well-being and our insurance." She said.

"You do know that you are the only person who could find humor in me being in a mental institution?" I asked her.

"Nope. No I'm not." Said Santina.

"You're going to make me start crying laughing." I told her.

"Good Rochelle." She replied. "Now you know what to do."

I knew the answer to the question I never knew to ask and the answer was me standing here in this place crying tears of joy.

Epilogue

Sandy Beaches- Elegy

She, was born in the cool Midwest during the month of February.

As bold and vulnerable as a thrashing wave rolling under water gliders, crashing and being consumed into the sand.

She, nurtured by the souls of freedom and conductors of this railroad, she became a freedom rider of life.

Sleep on sandy beaches little sister. #SayHerName #SandraBland

Afterword

Missing the TEARS, she cries:

Ever been in a room where everyone thinks you have your shit together? Standing at a podium delivering that awesome speech, sitting at your desk conducting a staff meeting or at your child's school leading the PTA meeting. There they all are, watching your every move, listening to your every word, agreeing with every suggestion you make. But they missed it.

You are out with your girls. The ones who claim to REALLY know you. Even getting dressed together at someone's house, they bring bottles and snacks for the wardrobe changing session. You try on different dress, shoe and accessory combinations and deliver a strut worthy of New York Fashion week. Your pre-party gathering is fun, festive and fabulous on your level. They are loving every moment of sister space, where no topic is off limits. Conversations about men, kids and coworkers are flowing. Some good, some bad, some even ugly. But they all end in laughter. But even they miss it.

A night out with the man of your dreams! You know the one that makes you feel all warm inside and seems to treat you like a queen. The who was raised right! That one who does and says all the right things to make you soul happy. He opens doors, orders the right wine, arranges to have flowers delivered and even finds a restaurant where your favorite band is playing. YES, all the things that scream, "You are surely going to get some tonight!"

You couldn't possibly ask for a better man in your life. He prides himself in making you smile. All his "boys" take tips from him and all your "girls" wish they had such a doting man. But somehow, he STILL missed it.

What about the family reunion where all the cousins are beaming with joy and pride when they see you? They greet you with such enthusiasm and unconditional love. Everyone is all smiles, taking selfies, sharing pics from special events and fixing plates of your favorite foods. The DJ even plays your favorite song, and everyone knows you can't resist the dance floor! There is a roar of laughter and chatter combined with hand clapping and feet tapping on the temporary dance floor laid under the tent. The elders watch with pure satisfaction at what they perceive as a job well done. You are the highlight of the family unit, The apple of their eyes. But they too missed it. Because all you really want to do is cry.

Hiding the TEARS, she cries

You, standing by, reeling in your self-inflicted heartache. It's the tiniest details, the smallest signals that the ones who are closest to her might miss. They get the big stuff. Remembering that time, you dated the guy the all hated? He was tall, dark and handsome. But he was also mean, abusive and a drunk. You've always been so good at hiding your pain. They'll never guess how awful it was! No one liked him but you couldn't figure out why. After all, you were running your best cloak and dagger show. You made sure you showed up to events together, even wore matching colors. You know those cheesy Christmas cards with a picture of the two of you looking blissfully happy? Yup! Did that too. Oh yes, and the Facebook page with pics of you two on vacations, date night and those summer concerts! Who wouldn't love you as a couple? This love looks amazing to the masses. But inside, she's enduring torture daily. Dam, they are missing it!

You worked so hard to conjure up that image that would make everyone love him... even though he didn't deserve it. Even though they said it, you know... "there is just something about his man that I don't like/", you continued to sing his praises. How could they know? Like that night at your best friend's birthday party. Of Course, he would want to go! He golf's with her man. They are friends. He'd definitely have someone to talk to there. So, first the invitation. Your hands are all sweaty as you walk up the stairs, down the hall and face the closed bedroom door. You've convinced yourself that this time, he'll be cool. Just sell the fact that HIS friend will be there. Not that you are dragging him out with your circle of cackling hen girlfriends this time. He must have heard you come up the stairs, so he yells out." Babe?" as if he is wondering why you haven't reported to his quarters yet. Instead of responding from the other side of the door, you quickly open is and smile at him. "Hey baby" you yell out as you go straight to the walk-in closet to change out of your work clothes and into your yoga pants and a sports bra. You hear him yelling at the TV while you study every imperfection on your body in the mirror. Why couldn't you just be beautiful and perfect?

He is knee deep in some sports thing of course, the 1st sign that it's not a good time to talk. You are thinking, not while he is watching sports, or the news, or his favorite TV sitcom. As you emerge from the walk-in closet in your workout gear, he says, "Guess dinner is take-out tonight again huh?" That's sign number 2. He hates it when you go to yoga because he doesn't go with you even though he has been invited. He prefers the sweaty meat market basketball gym that you hate to go to. But then acts a fool when someone is talking to you while you are on the treadmill. Gosh, doesn't he realize that doesn't happen at yoga? Shit! Do you go to yoga and have drama all night or skip it and fix dinner tonight? Of Course, dinner it is! Though in the fridge is ½ the lasagna you cooked last night and a huge container of grilled BBQ chicken from the weekend that he won't eat! So, you cook skipping yoga in hopes he would be more open to the party invitation. So, dinner is done, the table is set, and you are sitting in your yoga pants and sports bra at the table. You've texted him and yelled upstairs that dinner is ready at least 10 minutes ago. At the 12-minute mark you hear his feet, your hands get sweaty again, but you've got to tell him and get it over with. You can't miss the party. If you start talking about it today, he'll hopefully be willing by Friday. They're still missing it.

The conversation goes as expected. He doesn't want to go. You are always planning his time. The wonderful dinner you cooked is barely touched. He storms off knocking your sorority plague to the ground and kicks the basket of clean clothes in the hallway over. So, you spring into action, planning the other times, details and even wardrobe for your future attempts at this invite. Meanwhile you are taking yours and his clothes for the party to the dry cleaner. You stay optimistic or at least prepared, just in case You guys are known for your matching outfits. In your mind it keeps up the ideas that you are love birds and life is great in paradise. They have no idea that it takes you a week to convince him to come, Monday its no yoga and dinner, by Wednesday is getting to work late because he insist you have sex just as you are putting the key in the door to leave for the day. You are dressed for work but if you love him, you'll go to work smelling like him he says. Then Thursday its play nice in front of his friends for Thursday night football. You play the role as he treats you like the maid to prove to his friends that he has you in check. Is this how it's always going to be?

You do it all in hopes that he will agree to go to the party Friday night. Friday morning, he rewards you by allowing you to suck his penis to completion while you're in the bathroom getting dressed for work. But you talk it of course, all in the hopes of a favorable response. You make his lunch, decorated with a love note. Kisses till tonight when we dance the night away. Hoping that will warm him up to the idea. You text him at lunch: can't wait till tonight. Have you talked to Marc about the party? Hoping tying it in with his friends will soften him up. But, no response. You leave work and head to the dry cleaners to pick up your clothes for tonight. 1 outfit for you and 3 for him, so he has a choice of course. Did you make the right choices?

You get home to find his car is not in the driveway. You text him as a reminder, praying he doesn't let you down. He finally shows up 30 minutes after the party started. He has been to the gym and is on an adrenaline high. He needs you to beg, plead and please him before you go. It is now 2 hours into the party before you pull off and on to the charade. All to keep up the facade. You are exhausted and not even happy to be here, but you made it to the party. But. all you really want to do is cry.

Fighting the TEARS, she cries

It's the big day! At Least she hopes it is. Hard work pays off foes it? Well she is hoping, praying, counting on today to be the day that adage comes to fruition. It's been weeks of long hours, writing, editing and restarting the project of her dreams. The success of this presentation will springboard her career. She's educated and in debt. She's well read and unpublished. She's traveled the world yet has never seen any of the wonders of the world. But who would know other than her? Her friends, or maybe acquaintances marvel at her lifestyle. She is the star of her firm, the go to girl! And today is the big day!

She walks into the staff lounge and the buzz she heard outside the door turns to silence. She walks into her office just in time to catch a rainbow in the sky. So, cliché, but she'll take it as a sign of good luck! It's pregame show! As she checks the list off, her confidence abounds. Power suit, check. Comfortable yet stylish shoes, check. Race neutral hair style, check. Pale clear nail polish, check! The long night with her stylist and nail tech last night was well worth it. She's feeling herself, feeling great and feels her life is exactly where she wants it.

The next person who walks in her door is her assistant, her best friend and confidant. She walks in and takes a double take. Wait! She's thinking about what happened to her bestie! This power player sounds like her but looks nothing like her. Their conversation leads to a deep reflection about who she really is? Is the only way to climb the ladder embedded in the mainstream imagery? Is being racially, socially and professionally ambiguous and non-threatening the only way to secure this promotion? She will soon find out. She walks in and out of the boardroom in what seemed like a blink of an eye. Somehow, ever her drastic transformation did not make the desired impact.

She stares at herself in the mirror of the executive restroom where she has locked herself in after hearing the exact opposite of what she wanted to hear. Do they know what it takes to straighten out locs without making your hair fall out? Did they notice she did where any Afrocentric garb today? (The first time in months). No comments about her plant-based lifestyle or 3am meditation call today. She can hear her bestie's voice saying, "Just be you, do you and they will love you." But what happens when you've lost you? You find yourself morphed into the representative you think is most likely to be accepted. Then like an atomic bomb hitting your foundation, you realize they really don't care about who YOU are, present yourself to be or would like to be. At the end of the day, you are NOT one of them! You work until they put you out of the building, you've missed important family engagements, you're not even active in your sorority anymore? All part of your targeted plan and road to your promotion. But in the end, you still don't have a seat at that table. They won't let you in. As if selling out, or selling your soul was not enough.

As you come out of your reflection buried in your own thoughts, you look up at your reflection. You are looking at a stranger. Remembering the quieted buzz from the staff lounge, snickers in the main office and lowering of eyes in the elevator. As if they knew. Today was not going to be the day. But moreover, will there ever be a day? In that moment a tear fell which was quickly wiped away and pulled back. "Get it together! You got this! Trying your best to convince yourself that you did have it together and you will get another opportunity. While deep inside, all she wanted to do was cry.

ACCEPTING the TEARS, she cries

It's finally Friday at five. She closes the day of remote work, thankful that she didn't have to face her colleagues until next week. The doorbell rings just in time. It must be her grocery and wine delivery she ordered for girls' night in. After the last couple of weeks, her girls, her Homegirls are just what the doctor ordered. Talking trash, drinking wine, eating fried food is exactly what is needed to heal the soul. The men are gone, kids are handled, and agendas are cleared for the night. The homegirls will be eating in, drinking in and staying in. Just like a deck of cards, her Homegirls area full house! One who has her finance game tight. She lives well, married well and is well most of the time. One who is sound in her sexuality, sexuality and superwomaness. The other is adventurous, she lives life with no boundaries and unapologetically. She is a force to be reckoned with! Then there is her dot your eyes and cross your tees homegirl. She leaves no stone unturned and assures everyone is one point. You'd better not have her guessing about you because she will check you! And then there is her, me. The one who is just stepping into her homegirlness. Finding herself, making her mark and fitting her peg in the correct hole. The one that is custom made for me. She is finding the space where she feels supported enough to release her cry.

I cry tears for who everybody thinks I am, when I don't know myself.

I cry tears for the place I hold in my family, realizing it is a heavy burden.

I cry tears for the failed relationship I refused to let go in fear of judgement and loneliness.

I cry tears for helping someone else live their dreams, while mine remain dormant.

I cry tears for the culture I left behind to assimilate into the mainstream.

I cry tears for the children I had with the wrong man and the right man I never had children with.

I cry tears for the loss of self in the midst of my transformation.

With glasses half full, plates of food half eaten, music blasting and each of us with our own box of tissue, we cry, HOMEGIRL style. These are the type of tears that blind you and clear your insight simultaneously. These tears a cradled with the love, respect and genuine support that we seek in places they don't exist. So now she cries, because she has finally found the place where she CAN cry.

SHARING the TEARS, she cries

In the coming pages, I hope you find your person. The you among the

HOMEGIRLS who have all found a place that is safe to cry. The value of the cry is enumerable, yet seen as counter indicative of strength, courage, bravery and love. This book will reveal how wrong that idea is. As you move through the stories of these women who find each along their journey of self-actualization, look for yourself, your sister, your bestie among them. This story is one that demonstrates the fluidity of womanhood and friendship. As human beings, we go through a series of developmental milestones before we reach or pinnacle. To that end, you will find the friendships developed among these women is pivoted. It spins on an axis that is shifted by moods, moments and movements in their lives.

There is a natural evolution from girlfriends to homegirls that positions each of them toward their goals. Their conversations and experiences are incredible woven in and out various aspects of each other's lives. All with the common thread of self-improvement, self-determination and self-discipline. The characters are developed in a very relatable way. You know someone like her. You may even know her. You might even BE her. In the end, they all find the answer to the question. As they move deeper and deeper into the HOMEGIRL circle, they take with them what the previous HG shared with the purpose of passing it on. So now, we share with you the answer the question; "Where do Black Girls Go to Cry?" And once you've found your place, don't hold on to it selfishly. Share it and pass it on. Now go on girl. Go ahead and cry girl!

About the Author

Alicia Nicole *Mother, Author, Entrepreneur* , CEO

Alicia Norman was born in Chicago, Illinois. She was raised in Bolingbrook, a suburb of Illinois until age 18, and returned to Chicago after attending Howard University in 2005. After almost, ten years of working in the field of Information Technology and Project Management, and with much desire to provide quality reading books for her young son, she began writing his bedtime stories. Her first published book, "Good Night, I Love You, See You In The Morning, " was the first of her book series, "AOKA Books." Named after her son, "The Adventures of King Aidan."

After many of her own crisis situations and a rescue mission of her own, Alicia sought out to write a fictional story based on her own life that would inspire girls, women, Black girls and women, globally, to live in their purpose and recover from their own trauma, no matter how difficult a task it may seem. While writing this book, she called on her closest friends, mentors, and homegirls for guidance and support. Many are featured in her story.

Meet The Homegirls

Julie S Doar-Sinkfield *Mother,Editor, Contributing author, COO*

Julie Doar-Sinkfield co-wrote the initial charter application and two subsequent charter amendments for WEDJ PCS. She is responsible for overall policy development, strategic planning, reporting, fundraising and growth of the new public charter school. She has managed three construction projects, negotiated financing for two construction projects, and raised over $800,000 in grants and donations since opening. Her experience includes negotiating cash flow credit lines, establishing school credit history and securing a permanent location for the main campus in the initial year of operation. Ms. Doar-Sinkfield supervised school growth from one campus with 153 PreK through 5th grade students and 23 staff in 2004 to three campuses and 630 PreK through 12th grade students in 2010. She successfully coordinated school Accreditation in its 4th year. Prior to founding the William E. Doar, Jr. PCS, Ms. Doar-Sinkfield was first the Interim Principal and then the Program Development Specialist at Children's Studio School PCS, also in the District of Columbia. She was also Director of the Southeast Academy of Scholastic Excellence PCS in the District and the Middle School Director of The Newport School in Kensington, MD.

Ms. Doar-Sinkfield holds broad instructional experience in a variety of academic settings and grade levels. In addition, she volunteered with the National Hemophilia Foundation to present workshops to newly diagnosed families and created curricula to support the First Step – New Family Education Program. She has completed Parents Empowering Parents training and is a facilitator for both PEP and First Step.

Currently she works as an adjunct online professor of Sociology for Strayer University and Broward Community College.

Nadia Casseus Torney *Mother, Educator, Contributing Author, CPO*

Nadia Casseus Torney has an extensive background in the field of education. She has excelled in delivery of social and academic services to children in traditional as well as specialized settings for over 20 years.

She is a co-author of an initial application that was funded to open a Public Charter School in the District of Columbia and subsequently served as Co-Founder, Principal and Chief Academic Officer. Her tenure at the Public Charter was proceeded by Administrative positions at SouthEast Academy Public Charter School, The Children's Guild and National Children's Center. Her expertise extends from academic to clinic services. She served a supervisor for Related Services providers for the DCPS Office of Special Education. She mobilized advocacy campaigns for charter schools in the District of Columbia, New York and Maryland. A few of her distinguished achievements include successful grant writing; culminating in the funding of multi-million dollar state and national programs, serving as an educational consultant to Maryland's State Charter Advocacy Agency, several media appearances and numerous national speaking engagements.

Nadia's talents have afforded her the opportunity to serve as an adjunct professor at Johns Hopkins University of Baltimore and Trinity University in Washington DC. She is a national certified trainer for the American Federation of Teachers and has developed a series of professional development modules for The Washington Teachers' Union.

Nadia currently serves as an Administrator at a District of Columbia Public school where she continues to train, coach and mentor educators and service providers to the children with the most severe needs.

Santina Brown *Entrepreneur,Member of the Armed Forces, Contributing author, CRO*

Santina Brown is a very versatile, reliable, and efficient professional with 13+ years of experience in finance. She combines academic training in business administration with hands-on experience in budgeting, logistics, and accounting support to offer employers a system to efficiently account for funds within each contributing department. Developed ability to problem solve and prioritize, achieving goals in diverse and challenging environments.

You can connect with me on:

- https://www.internationalhomegirls.com
- https://twitter.com/AAliciaNicole
- https://facebook.com/TheRealAlicianicole

Also by Alicia Nicole Norman

Good Night, I Love You, See You In The Morning

The perfect bedtime story for the child that doesn't want to go to sleep. Discover, with your child, the many ways King Anthony can come up with to avoid bedtime. This playful, fun, and cute story is just what the tired parent needs to turn bedtime into story time. Enjoy the bedtime story of King Anthony and his mom, one energetic five year old who refuses to go to sleep and his caring mother. This story is sure to make your little one laugh and giggle as they try to figure out how King Anthony plans to stay awake!

King, Mom, and Mommy

A loving story about a young boy who learns that his family is different. Written in a poetic voice, the author shows the reader the love from two non-traditional parents for their child. As we learn the story of how King Aidan was born, we grow to adore him as a normal, funny, and inquisitive little boy.

www.ingramcontent.com/pod-product-compliance
Lightning Source LLC
Chambersburg PA
CBHW070630310726
48982CB00001B/233

* 9 7 8 0 6 9 2 1 9 7 7 0 7 *